Solitude's End

An Echo's Way Adventure

Mike Waller

SOLITUDE'S END

Copyright © 2017 by Michael D. Waller

This novel is entirely a work of fiction. The names, characters and incidents portrayed in it are the work of the author's imagination. Any resemblance to actual persons, living or dead, events or localities is entirely coincidental.

Michael D. Waller asserts the moral right to be identified as the author of this work.

First edition
Published by Rampart Publishing 2017
ISBN: 9780994438690

The 'ECHO'S WAY' Adventures

The ECHO'S WAY stories relate the adventures of Echo Bourke, a remarkable young woman who finds herself embroiled against her will in the harsh reality of a war between the Federation of Humanity and a powerful alien neighbor, the Tolleani.

Each Book is a separate adventure, rather than part of a continuing, single story. There are no 'to be continued's and no cliff-hangar endings. Each book can be read as a stand-alone story in the life of our heroine.

Solitude's End is the first adventure in Echo Bourke's journey, and tells of how she survives an alien attack as a teenager, and thus is set on the path to a future she could never have imagined.

This book utilizes U.S. English spelling.

Chapter One

DUST SWIRLED IN GENTLE breaths as air wafted across the tarmac and scattered the dry leaves blown in from the surrounding forest during the night. The early morning sun was fierce, normal for the planet Corros but more so than usual on this particular day. The regular morning sea breeze had failed to arrive on time, and the oppressive humidity sucked the will from anyone unwise enough or with no option but to be active at that hour.

Outside one of the hangars, a maintenance vehicle eased in beside a line of refuse containers, and the operator jumped to the ground. One of a handful of workers out at this early time of the day, he set to the task of guiding full bins to the hydraulic lift of his truck. The sudden high-pitched whine of engines reached his ears, the sounds of a ship high above the airfield. He scanned the sky, squinting in the bright morning haze and wondering who they might be. No arrivals were scheduled for today, so whoever the approaching craft belonged to, they were unexpected.

A beam of intense, shimmering, blue light lanced down from the low cloud, reducing the truck's cab to a melted tangle of fused and burning metal. A second blast left a black, steaming ash pile where the driver once stood. A siren wailed to alert the base personnel to the attack, and within seconds, half-dressed but fully armed men rushed from the barracks, desperately searching for their invisible assailant. Each man collapsed as scintillating beams of destruction lashed down from the unseen source high in the cloud cover.

***

Two sleek strike-fighters sat at the edge of the landing field, their pitch-black, light-absorbing fuselages mere shadows in the hazy morning light. The deadly-looking machines were the principal defense provided by the military for the colonists on this world, their streamlined hulls and stubby wings making them capable of flight in both atmosphere and space.

Barbus Koll, Sub-Flight-Controller of Tollean Stealth-Task-Force Three, eased forward in his seat and savored the moment's magic as he tightened a well-manicured finger on the trigger. He had not had so much fun in a long time.

From beneath Koll's ship, a radiant, blue beam lanced down and slammed into the alien vessel on the airfield below. A child-like chuckle escaped his lips as one of the once-deadly enemy spacecraft became a melted monument of harmless metal and plastic. A follow-up shot left the second ship, parked beside the first, in an equivalent state. He congratulated himself and eased back in his seat, the claws of one foot tapping out a vague, discordant rhythm on the plates of the cockpit foot-well.

Too easy, he thought.

It eluded him why these human creatures warranted such a waste of effort, but one had to enjoy oneself whenever the opportunity arose, and he so enjoyed the act of blatant destruction.

The fleeting moment of elation faded as his mind slid back to normality. Below, the volume of returning fire decreased as the survivors continued to scuttle like insects across the tarmac, firing their weapons futilely into the clouds. Not that they posed any threat; Koll's squadron flew higher than the handguns of the humans could reach, even had they been able to see his ships through the cloud layer.

Damn this planet, he thought. If he found any place repugnant, it was one of these yellow-star worlds. The intense light and the heat made his eyes water, and everything about the place annoyed him. Official policy dictated that the Empire might need the resources this world offered, and even the second-rate human infrastructure might be useful, so his superior insisted on a minimum of unnecessary destruction. Given a choice, Koll would pound the base to dust from high orbit.

No such restriction applied to the specific target below, a military base intended to protect the colony. As the leader of a squad of nine one-man fighters, Koll's appointed task was to sneak in and shut down communications and defenses before the enemy detected the alien force's arrival. The planet's satellites, and the dishes and towers around the base, had been his first priority; he could not allow any warning of this attack to leak to the other settlements on the planet. At this moment, the larger mother ship would be approaching orbit and would soon dispatch troop shuttles to complete the take down of the mining facilities themselves.

The nearest actual mine and the airstrip servicing it were five kilometers away at the head of a deep valley in the nearby mountains. The town attached to the operation lay behind the coastal dunes a short distance to the east, and its closeness to this airbase made it the world's principal commercial center and the next objective in this cleansing exercise. Each of the attack fighters under Koll's command was able to level the colony alone if necessary, but Tollean imperial forces rarely worked that way. The preferred strategy always involved overwhelming force for the simplest of operations.

Koll felt he had performed his assigned mission with superb efficiency, as usual. Tasked with the specific job of neutralizing the enemy military response, he had achieved the objective with just two shots. The ships on the tarmac below would never fly again.

Positioned high up for safety, his squad quartered the base, easily cleaning up the remaining human figures that milled around the field. Infrared detection made it simple to pinpoint individual targets, including those inside the buildings, and pick them off with needle beams while remaining safe above the clouds. These settlements had no heavy armaments, and the weapons they did possess were incapable of damaging the shielded hulls of the Tollean space forces. The humans were helpless without the protection of their warships.

Koll raised a hand to shelter his eyes from the harsh morning light and looked out towards the township just visible beyond the distant dunes. The massive, bulky shapes of troop carriers descended, hovering over the buildings. As they touched down, ramps dropped from the stern of each, and ground troops poured out, ignoring the cries of the human animals as they proceeded to clear the settlement and shoot down every soul regardless of sex or age. The task was straightforward, and Koll expected it would not take long.

The less time spent on this miserable planet, the better, he thought.

The clearance of the mine presented a bigger problem than the attack on the space field or town. With all workings underground, soldiers had no choice but to enter the tunnels, tedious and time-wasting work, but not difficult. Koll did not care. He would not have to go into the shafts. In a few hours, no alien would remain alive, no matter where it hid.

The war against humanity was still in its infancy, and so far, the Emperor's forces had met with little resistance. Koll found it hardly surprising. The only other intelligent species ever encountered, humans had first come to the attention of the Tolleani almost three hundred years ago when a solitary ship entered a star system on the fringe of Tollean influence. That vessel had been destroyed, sent crashing onto a rocky world so high in gravity it was considered useless by the bureaucracy.

Humans were civilized to a point, but Koll saw them as little more than smart animals, and their technological advances in no way compared with the great achievements of the

Empire. In reality, the two races might have coexisted, as the humans tended to occupy warm, watery worlds orbiting yellow or orange stars, while Koll's species preferred cooler planets around red-dwarf suns. However, to the Tollean mindset, the idea of sharing the galaxy with inferior beings was unthinkable.

There was also the matter of resources. Destined to last forever, the Empire would someday need all the wealth it could obtain, but the human morass was now expanding at an existential rate and threatened to be a serious competitor in this part of the galaxy. A unilateral decree from the Emperor required the problem to be dealt with permanently—a non-existent rival posed no threat.

These colonies mined Aspolin 43—the humans referred to it as Trilatenite—and the mineral's presence on this world was the sole reason for this campaign. The greatest prize of all, it alone made interstellar travel possible. Several Empire worlds possessed vast quantities of the substance, making this planet superfluous for now, but in the future, anything was possible. The enemy had a less-ready supply, and the loss of the mining colony would limit their ability to resist the relentless Tollean war machine.

Regardless of immediate needs, the mission directive was to leave this world empty. The invasion force employed a scorched-world policy, leaving no human alive as the front advanced. Not a problem, Koll thought. His team excelled at that task.

Beyond the town, troop carriers lifted off and turned towards the mine site. Koll sent two of his fighters to accompany them; he doubted they would be needed, but one could never be too sure.

Several of the large hangars at the rear of the base, one of which was in flames, showed severe damage. Other structures had fared worse. Many human targets were destroyed by shooting down through the roofs, setting fire to insulation, and leaving more than half the buildings ablaze. Only a handful stood untouched, including a small building near the entrance, several unoccupied maintenance structures around the perimeter, and a few storage units.

In a far corner of the field, one of the smallest hangars appeared undamaged, so Koll flew his ship lower and hovered over the building, curious to see if anything there might be of interest. No heat signatures appeared within, so after a moment's pause, he decided to leave it intact. There was no telling what he might find inside, and orders must be obeyed.

Within reason.

For Koll, the term 'unnecessary destruction' was relative, dependent on his ability to explain his actions to his superior. He enjoyed destroying things, but too much senseless damage could easily result in a black mark on his record.

All around, burned and charred bodies lay scattered where they fell, and no movement disturbed the field. Satisfied the resistance had ended, Koll ordered all but one of his squad to land. After landing his vessel, he jumped to the ground and waited as the polarizers on his helmet adjusted.

Hmm, hot and humid, as expected, he thought.

These humans chose to live in the worst kinds of environments. The brilliant sunlight blinded Koll, and waves of shimmering heat rose from the hard-baked surface. The temperature here was intolerable, the humidity oppressive, and the air stank of ozone from the attack. Drawn by the smell of death, a plague of insects swarmed over the base, but then ignored the alien bodies and instead attacked Koll and his men the second they stepped from their ships.

Thankful for his armor's protection from the worst of the annoying pests, he directed his team to check the buildings and rout any enemy hiding where heat detectors could not find them. As the soldiers dispersed, he strolled towards the undamaged hangar.

At the front of the structure, a small personnel entrance, secured with a heavy steel padlock, stood to one side of the main portal. Koll contemplated the massive doors for a moment, then raised his handgun and shattered the lock on the smaller access with a single blast. Weapon at the ready, he entered. The lights were off, with the only illumination coming from translucent panels on the roof. Shadows shrouded the gloomy interior.

At the center of the floor, a sleek, matte-black ship stood amidst a maze of maintenance machinery. The condition of the vessel was obvious. One engine was disconnected, with various component pieces scattered on service benches around the hull.

A glance through the open hatch showed the helm console in disarray, wires and cables hanging down in tangled confusion. It was clear the craft was not space-worthy in its

current state of disrepair, but neither was it damaged—just inoperable due to the maintenance activities.

Koll's mind ticked over at an increasing pace, counting the ways he might benefit from this discovery. The black, light-absorbing hull marked the ship as a Federation military vessel. Unarmed, it posed no threat to the invasion force, but the possibility existed that it might be useful for clandestine operations. With the two ships outside beyond repair, this one might serve as an appeasement for the Flag Controller, and he might well show extra favor. One never knew.

Minutes later, Koll stood once more beneath the wings of his ship, listening to reports on his helmet radio. The rout of the town was almost complete, soldiers at the mine were entering the shafts, and this phase of the operation would soon be over. Without military support, the second settlement, one hundred kilometers inland, was defenseless, and ground troops alone would suffice. A short distance south along the coast, all the facilities at the third site were centered on a single location, and again, a small force would easily suffice to take out the lot.

Koll decided to divide his remaining ships, sending three each to the second and third mine sites. With no more military opposition, his role was to supervise and provide backup as needed. He cursed the heat and the insects once again as he climbed back into his ship's cool cockpit and slammed the hatch.

This place disgusted him.

Chapter Two

IT WAS THE BEST season of the year, but not today. At thirty-five degrees centigrade, the atypical Corros spring day was a little hotter than usual, and thanks to the always-present humidity, only just bearable.

Cinta Bourke, known to her family and friends as Echo, stepped down from the verandah to the gravel path at the front of the house. With a quick wave of farewell over her shoulder to her mother, she walked to the yard gate, her school satchel slung over her shoulder.

As the daughter of the manager of the small mining facility of Casta, Echo had grown up in this place, and life had been charmed, so far. Her father, as the mine chief, was the power here. Mother, whom she adored, was the opposite, a calm, collected, and long-suffering woman who lived life intent on raising both her children as models of perfection, but with little success: Echo and her younger brother possessed minds of their own.

She peered along the dirt road towards the central square where the schoolhouse was located. Everyone in the town considered Echo a bright girl; for her, learning was a passion, and she loved school.

"Too smart for a place like Corros," her teachers often said.

At seventeen standard years of age, her childhood was almost over, and with final assessments just a week away, she would soon graduate and take her place in society.

Young girls generally went to work in the town facilities or the mine offices, or tended the crops and stock. Expected to marry within a year or two of finishing school, they became homemakers and mothers at an early age, caring for the next generation of colonists and helping their husbands cope with a difficult and dangerous existence. Echo considered it almost feudal, and many of the colonists agreed, both men and women, but such was the reality of the perimeter mining colonies. Many women became widows at an early age.

On this world, most of the boys left school to apprentice in the mines, a dangerous job leading to an oftentimes short life span. They would become hard men, dedicated to their occupation, with a pride born from the knowledge that the dirty, gray rock they mined kept the Federation functioning and the interstellar spaceships flying. In recent years, a few of them had gone away to train for the military because of the war, but most remained. The work of the mining communities was critical to civilization and the war effort.

Echo sometimes dreamed of moving to one of the bigger cities on a primary world, perhaps Cymbel 3 or Tantalus, the prime world of the Federation. Perhaps even Old Earth. No, perhaps not there. Word was that the origin planet was environmentally unhealthy, and only career politicians and bureaucrats made that choice, choosing advancement in the vast Federation machine over personal well-being.

Echo accepted it was unlikely she would ever see any of the prime worlds. In a place like Corros, the life choices of a young woman, even one as intelligent as her, remained limited.

She hesitated by the gate. The merciless sun sent small heat ripples dancing into the air as it beat down upon the roadway. At this time of year, rain fell only in the evening or at night. For most of the daylight hours, the temperature and humidity made concentration in class difficult, and today was shaping up to be worse than normal. The school had no air conditioning, and the usual daytime breeze from the nearby ocean was late this morning.

On an impulse, Echo peeked over her shoulder to make sure her mother had gone inside, then turned and walked in the opposite direction from the town center, towards the watercourse that skirted the edge of the settlement.

The last few weeks had involved constant study. Echo knew the exam material as well as she ever would and had no concerns about her ability to pass the final assessments. Under the circumstances, some free time struck her as more appropriate than sweltering all morning in a hot room for no reason. She would attend the afternoon classes with a story about helping her mother.

Excuses like that were common. In this town, education always came second to the realities of life. The teacher would never dare doubt her, with her father the boss of mining operations and therefore the most prominent figure in the community. Even the mayor deferred to him. Of course, her father would never condone skipping classes if he knew about it. He was a fair but strict man who believed strongly in the value of education, even in a backwater like Casta.

The stream along the far side of the fields provided water for the town, crops, animals, and the mine, and served as a popular source of relaxation for the younger inhabitants. Around one side of the town, waterholes, some natural and others created by small dams, were scattered every few hundred yards.

To reach the stream, Echo cut across the market gardens. The crops, products of the finest genetics laboratories of the Federation, flourished in this alien environment despite the biology of this world being marginally incompatible with Terran life forms.

Echo's favorite swimming spot was at the base of the high rocky ridge beyond the airfield, a quiet, deep pool surrounded by shady trees, where the water tumbled down from the dam and power station in the higher gorges of the surrounding, shattered mountains. It was a perfect place for spending the morning, and with her friends in class, she had it to herself.

With school clothes folded and placed on a dry rock, she slid into the clear, cool water. Nothing gave her more joy than swimming, and she often wondered how she would cope without access to places like this. In the severe humidity, the cold caress of the mountain pool was most enjoyable, the chill touch on her skin almost luxurious as she eased herself in.

The spot was elevated about fifty meters above the airfield tarmac, and as she lay in the shallows at the outflow, Echo looked out towards the distant mining compound located between the airfield and the town. Her father's office was visible, and she prayed he would not spot her. His doing so would mean an unpleasant scene when she returned home.

At the back of the compound, beyond a broad apron, the entrance tunnel to the workings was visible. The Casta mine was one of three on Corros that mined Trilatenite. At first glance, the raw ore looked like any other rock, but the processed metal was essential in the construction of fusion reactors and the gateway generators that allowed access to interstellar wormholes. Father once told her the dull, silver-gray ore had formed the basis of numerous fortunes and ruined even more good souls. Rare in most human-occupied planetary systems, the substance was the only reason, her father maintained, that the Federation built settlements way out here at all.

Floating on her back in the shallow water, she stared up into the treetops. The faintest of ripples stirred through the branches, bringing hope that the much-missed morning breeze had at last arrived to relieve the humidity.

Small, bird-like creatures flitted through the canopy, dropping down on leathery wings to flap around in the shallow water of the pool. Named Pterosaurs after an ancient creature of Old Earth, they were indigenous to this world and grew to enormous sizes. Only the smaller ones came to the pools, but even the largest gave no concern to the colonists. Few of the native animals on the planet ever caused problems; Corros was a benign world.

Without warning, the little creatures took wing and fled, spooked by a loud rumble from the direction of the coastal dunes. Echo watched, puzzled, as five spaceships descended over the town and settled onto the airfield.

Two large, wide-bodied machines landed first, and within seconds, hatches sprang open, and armored soldiers flooded out, forming lines in front of the two buildings beside the airfield gate. The remaining three craft, smaller and sleeker in appearance, hovered above the field for a few minutes before settling beside their larger companions.

Three workers emerged from the door of the airfield office, but before they could take another step, the new arrivals cut them down with laser fire. Echo's heart skipped a beat as she ducked low behind the rim of the pool. Only then did she comprehend. The colony was under attack, not by humans but by alien invaders.

The teachers in the school had often lectured the children about the Tolleani, the only other intelligent species encountered by humanity. Everyone knew about the current war but rarely spoke of it. Several Federation warships were stationed on Corros as a precaution, but nobody expected the aliens to bother with a small colony this far off the space lanes and so far from the Tollean home worlds.

They were wrong.

Lines of soldiers now stood on the tarmac. A handful of individuals broke away to search the hangars, while another small group stepped over the bodies of the slain men and entered the airfield office. Seconds later, they emerged and moved around to the smaller aircrew barracks. Echo knew it would be empty, as only the crews of the cargo transporters used that building when they arrived once a month to take away the ore.

The bulk of the troops turned and marched through the gate into the mine compound, a third of their number continuing to the town beyond. The remainder scattered among the work buildings or moved on towards the mine entrance.

Lasers flashed, and someone too distant for Echo to identify fell to the ground on the mine apron. With a subconscious swipe of a hand, she wiped away the tears streaming from her eyes. It was clear the invaders intended to murder everyone in the settlement, including her family and friends. Echo's day of peaceful relaxation descended into a nightmare, and a dull thud, the sound of her heart beating as the blood pounded in her temples, reverberated through her head. She realized she was gasping for breath, squeezed her eyes shut, and fought to control her hyperventilation.

On the tarmac below, a tall, thin alien jumped down from one of the smaller ships. He wore blue and green armor, different from the red and green of those routing the township, and something, an undefined arrogance in his stance, marked him as an officer. This, Echo thought, must be the leader of the invading force.

He paused for a moment beneath his ship, turning slowly to scan the airfield before he strolled across to the gate. Minutes later, he appeared again on the concourse near her father's office. Movement caught her attention as two soldiers dragged a man in front of the commander.

Dad!

Despite the distance, her father was easy to identify by his bright red shirt. He argued with the Tollean officer, who stood motionless without responding, and then, without warning, raised a pistol and shot the man's legs from beneath him. Echo stifled a scream, her hand over her mouth as her father collapsed to the ground. She knew instinctively the soldiers around the airfield hangars were close enough to hear her.

Her body shook uncontrollably as she pushed back from the lip of the outflow and swam to the back of the pool. Grabbing her clothes, she dressed and then picked her way down the stream bed. Thirty meters further on, she hesitated.

The alien task force numbered at least one hundred soldiers, all heavily armed. Without a weapon and with no chance of getting one, the odds that she, a teenage girl, could do anything at all to stop or hinder them were not worth consideration. If she went down to the town, she would die, so home was no longer an option. Sitting on a rock, she batted at the stream of tears and began to examine her alternatives.

"When in doubt, hide," her father always taught. "You lose a few minutes of your day, but if something's amiss, you gain time to think before you react. Leap in without thinking, and you die."

Turning aside, she scrambled into the thick brush at the back of the watercourse. Far under the trees, she crawled into a water-worn cavity in the face of a limestone outcrop. The rock shielded her from detection from above, but she was still close enough to hear when the aliens left. Curled up against the cool stone, she closed her eyes, her sobs so hard her lungs screamed in torture. She tried desperately to control the shaking of her body and waited for the sound of the departing ships.

* * *

Barbus Koll lifted his ship from the airfield and began a slow grid search, one eye fixed on the infrared readout. He did not expect to find anything and wondered why he bothered. The detectors could not locate a human inside the mine—not that there was anyone left alive down there—and the heat insulation in many of the structures interfered with the readings. In many places, the device was now useless, overloaded by the presence of nearby burning buildings. Most of the bodies scattered through the mine compound and the town still showed dull traces of a signature, but there was no movement.

None of this worried him in the slightest. The men had picked through each building and checked under the floors and above the ceilings, and Koll was satisfied that every human was dead.

He decided to make one last check before leaving and commenced a circuit of the outer edges of the valley in search of survivors hidden in the surrounding forest. Ten minutes later, he gave up. The job was complete, and the mine, per standard Tollean policy, remained intact in case of need by the Empire at some future time. He pulled back on the controls and sent his ship soaring up into the clouds towards the mother ship.

Good riddance, he thought.

Chapter Three

EVERYWHERE ECHO TURNED, SHE heard silence, bar only the whispering of the long-awaited breeze. Even the animals in the distant fields had gone quiet. Nothing moved, and bodies lay scattered on the concourse.

This was a massacre, not an attack, she thought.

For almost an hour, she stood at the gate between the airfield and the mine compound, unable to find the courage to proceed. Taking a deep breath, she forced one foot forward and began to walk towards her father's office.

How long she huddled at the back of the hollow she did not know, but eventually the roar of ships announced the invaders were leaving. The high-pitched whine of one of the smaller craft remained, growing softer then louder until at one stage it was overhead. That also faded in time, leaving only the sound of her sobbing.

Slowly, willing her rebellious legs to take a step at a time, she approached the body on the ground outside the mine office. It was indeed her father, the man she idolized, who had raised her with the love and devotion found only between father and daughter.

He was a massive man, but kind and gentle. Never in memory had a hand been raised in anger against her, her brother, or her mother. He loved them all without reservation, and Echo adored him in return.

On occasional trips to an old mining hut deep in the nearby mountain gorges, he taught her how to survive and live off the land, not an easy task on an alien world. Echo never understood why, but she had been happy to spend the time alone with him regardless. From him, she learned how to defend herself and rely on her own resources.

She had never needed to use the knowledge; the mere thought of what he would do to any man who touched his little girl served to keep her safe in this community. He was—had been—her favorite human being. She suspected he had always wanted her to be a boy. Now he was gone.

Echo took another swipe at the tears that stung her eyes, took a deep breath, and glanced down. Father was heavy. Burying him would not be easy, but she would find a way. Several other bodies lay nearby, and she expected more would be inside the buildings. She could not bury them all.

Long ago, when just a small child, she had been in the workings with her father, but she did not know the way alone, and the tunnels were treacherous. They frightened her. Any bodies there would remain untouched, the mine their tomb. As good as any, she thought, battling to get a handle on the moment.

The breeze began to pick up, dropping the humidity to a tolerable level. As Echo shuffled along the dirt road to the town, she almost convinced herself it was a normal spring afternoon. Only faint wisps of smoke rising from a handful of burnt buildings betrayed the truth of what had happened.

The village had fared no better than the compound. Bodies lay where they fell, and a deathly pall of silence hung over the once happy and bustling little community. Echo forced herself to disregard her eyes as she made her way towards her house. Father taught her to be strong, and she knew he would expect her to live up to his teachings.

As she walked by the school, she saw only death and destruction. She would not search for her brother yet; if he were alive, he would be home by now. If not…

There was no trace of him in the old homestead. Echo's mother lay in the front room, silent and alone, a small, neat laser burn on her forehead; Echo could do nothing but sit on the veranda, numbed by shock, her world awash with denial.

Rescue must surely arrive within the next few days. The ore carriers arrived every month, so they would be on their way now. Considering the distance between Corros and the primary worlds, they would not be aware of the attack and so would continue to come.

For hours, Echo rode a slippery slide to despair, her thoughts in turmoil and her chest aching from the wracking of her misery. Then, remembering her father's words, she scrambled to her feet, sucked in a deep breath and wiped the hair from her eyes. Shaking her arms and legs to drive away the numbness, she stepped down to the yard. There was work to do, and anything was better than dwelling on hopelessness.

Be strong, she told herself, and then wondered how the Gods could expect that of her.

Survival would be a concern for at least a short time, and a way had to be found to defend herself. If the attackers returned, she would not make the job easy for them. As a rule, weapons were barred from the mining colonies, but old Mister Bennett owned an antique pistol, and there was a laser rifle in her father's office for security purposes.

The bodies in the settlement needed attention; in the hot sun, they would soon begin to deteriorate. On this world, disease did not concern Echo. With the artificial immunity given to all colonists, nothing here could harm her, but decomposition would still pose problems.

Besides, leaving them where they lay was somehow improper; they deserved some kind of closure. Set on her first task, she walked around the house to the storage shed and fetched a shovel and hoe.

Digging was hard in the heat of the day, but Echo forced herself to keep working until the hole in the garden looked adequate. Perhaps it was not quite deep enough. It might have been a little longer for her father, but consumed by her misery, it was the best she could manage. It was not as wide as she would like, but it would serve.

She found her brother in the schoolyard. Teachers and children lay in small knots where the staff and some of the older students tried to protect the younger ones. Their attempts had been in vain. All had died.

By one mangled body she paused and sucked in air involuntarily, then collapsed to the ground, her vision blurring as her tortured emotions heaved once again. It was obvious that Jonathon, the only boy she had ever been close to, had attempted to fight back, and the attackers had cut him to pieces. For a moment, guilt wracked her mind, anger that she had not been here to help. Then she realized the truth: if she had, she would be lying beside her friend.

Determined to push on, she retrieved a canvas tarp from the school workshop and wrapped her baby brother's remains before taking him home.

Father was a different matter. Echo accepted that he would be difficult to move, but the machinery-filled compound soon offered a solution, a small gravel loader stored in a garage behind the workshops. Small enough for her to handle, it had a bucket scoop at the front large enough to carry her father. All she needed was the key.

The problems began when she turned the ignition. Never having driven a tracked vehicle before, or any with levers instead of a steering wheel, her first attempt to move the machine fractured the back wall of the shed. As she maneuvered forward, the corner of the scoop connected with the doorway, collapsing the frame onto the cab of the loader and causing almost terminal damage to the garage structure.

Once outside the ruined building, Echo spent fifteen minutes driving around the yard, backing up, turning, and learning which levers raised, lowered, and tilted the scoop. Satisfied that she would not kill herself, she drove out to the concourse and lined the loader up with her father's body, then tilted and lowered the scoop flat to the ground. Slowly and with great care, she rolled her father into the bucket, then raised it and drove the machine towards the town.

The following morning, Echo sat on the homestead veranda drinking a glass of fruit juice and contemplated her next course of action. Her chest still ached, but the tears were gone, replaced by a grim resolve. Overnight, her mind had calmed, faced with the harsh reality that she was now alone, possibly the only human left on Corros.

The previous evening, she had buried her father, mother, and brother together in the garden, planting three rough grave-markers made from tied stakes at their heads. Over the disturbed soil she placed rocks stolen from garden borders and roadway edges. The result did not satisfy, but exhausted as she was from a long, sleepless night of tossing, turning, and tears, nothing would.

As the sun rose higher over the town, she used the loader to take Jonathon's remains to his home, where she buried him with his mother. Of his father, there was no trace; the man was a shaft worker and was almost certainly somewhere below ground.

The townspeople were next on her agenda. Originally, she had intended to use the loader to dig a mass grave, but the experience of the previous day proved that impractical. Designed to carry loose fill, the scoop dug poorly, undoubtedly as much through lack of operator skill as the abilities of the machine.

It was impossible to bury everyone by hand, and for the rest, cremation seemed the simplest alternative. With the loader, she cleared the village center as much as possible and built a pyre in the square, setting the piled bodies ablaze with machine oil from the workshops.

Her mind numb and cold with resignation, she no longer acknowledged the horror of death; the bodies were cord wood, and not the friends with whom she had grown up. Unable to bear watching the flames, she left the pyre to its own devices and moved on.

The remaining victims, including those from the houses nearest the homestead, were collected and placed in piles on the roadways, again using oil to burn them. No doubt she had overlooked many of her fellow villagers: a scattering of buildings lay beyond the perimeter, and there would be workers in the fields.

After completing the job, she realized the remains of the fires would be obvious if the aliens returned, but that could not be helped. In that event, she had little chance of survival anyway, and at least she had given her people some closure.

The next day, noises from the stockyards alerted her to a problem she had not yet considered. Bellows of pain reached her ears as she ran towards the dairy. The cattle on Corros were hybrids adapted to digest the alien, grass-like vegetation on this world and produce vast quantities of milk. Dependent on humans, they required milking twice daily, and now the pressure building in their udders from several days of inattention was causing them pain.

At first, Echo thought to milk them—like almost everybody in the colony, she knew how—but then realized the impracticality of attending to fifty cows on her own. Soon she would be either leaving or dead, and nobody would tend to them when she was gone. Echo flinched at the thought of what she must do, but try as she might, she could see no alternative.

A short while later, she returned with the laser rifle from her father's office under her arm. Thirty petrifying minutes more, and the distressed creatures lay dead. Once again in tears, Echo returned to the veranda of the house, wondering if the dairy was far enough away to leave the carcasses where they lay. If the smell became a problem, the milking shed would have to burn.

Drained by her efforts, she felt something inside her had died. The cows were her favorite of all the farm animals, but her action was the only one possible under the circumstances.

Over the next few days, she dealt with the other animals. The beef cattle, pigs, and goats were released from their pens and paddocks, except for a small number kept in case of emergencies. The chickens, ducks, and turkeys also went free, again with a handful of exceptions. Echo knew the town had enough stored food to keep her alive for some time, but there was always a marginal chance that rescue would be longer in coming than expected.

Several days after the attack, satisfied she had done her best, she lay down on her bed and waited for the shaking to stop, not emerging for another twenty-four hours. Only then did the fact that she was completely alone hit her with full force. The thought overwhelmed her. A ship had to come soon.

* * *

No ship came. Unbeknownst to Echo, the next two ore-carriers to arrive were destroyed by Tollean ships still present in the system, before they could get anywhere near the planet. Only then did Fleet realize there had been a change of ownership of that star, and the continual stream of ore carriers and supply ships ceased.

On Cymbel 3, the prime world responsible for the administration of the colonies in that sector of space, the decision was made to close the Corros wormhole and set a guard. As vital as the mines were to the war effort, there were no resources available to respond, so for now the system would remain in Tollean hands.

Intelligence services on Cymbel failed to see any logical reason why the Tolleani would want that system, and finally determined that the invasion had been purely to destroy the mines and their supply of Trilatenite to humanity.

For now, the vital mineral would be a scarce resource, but given luck and a few years, the system would quieten down enough to allow a stealth ship to sneak in and begin the preliminary surveys necessary for a reciprocal invasion.

No thought was given to the inhabitants of Corros. The Tollean penchant for employing a scorched-world policy was well known, and it was doubtful anyone remained alive. As was so often the case, the decision not to send a rescue mission was determined by money, resources, and politics.

33

Chapter Four

Three years later.

ECHO RAISED HER EYES and peered up at the clouds. Surely that faint noise was the sound of a ship?

Nothing!

With a deep sigh, she returned her attention to the small plot of vegetables she maintained in one corner of the massive crop field behind her homestead.

After three years, she had almost given up thoughts of rescue. It was clear humanity had abandoned her, and that if she was to survive, it was up to her to make it alone.

At first, feelings of betrayal and abandonment overwhelmed her, and days of depression followed the final admission that she was on her own. In time, she accepted there was no one to hear her tears and rants, and life regained some sense of direction.

Now twenty years old by Federation standard time, she had accepted that the Tolleani most likely controlled this planetary system, and rescue would be difficult anyway.

Luckily, and with foresight, she had kept some of the chickens and goats and begun tending the corner of the market garden just beyond the back fence. Life continued, lonely and tedious, but never without hope. She sought always to prove her father right; she was made of better stuff.

Suddenly, the sound came again, this time the distinct roar of a ship. Looking up, Echo saw a vague, gray shape break through the low clouds, resolving to a bulky cargo shuttle as it cruised up from the coast. As it approached, a doubt hit Echo's mind. This one was not like the ore ships that used to come. It looked a lot like the troop shuttles she had seen on the airfield, the day of the invasion.

Crouching back under the spread of a fruit tree, she watched as the ship swooped over the town and the mine compound and settled beside one of the hangars.

The Tolleani were back!

Dropping her tools, she ran at a crouch to the back veranda of the house, where she retrieved a backpack. Realizing she would probably never be rescued, she had anticipated this event and kept an emergency pack ready at all times. Her father's advice echoed in her thoughts.

Grabbing the pack, she ran back to the field and made her way down to the creek. Minutes later, she disappeared without a trace into the dense vegetation that grew over the bank on the far side.

***

Base Coordinator Koll kicked a boot into the hard gravel and cursed loud enough to startle Under-Leader Brask, his second in command. The place was unchanged, the buildings a little run down through lack of maintenance over the years, but still serviceable with some work.

In the transport ship above, a scientific team was even now preparing to descend to the surface of Corros, their mission being to use this old human base for the development of a weapon intended to end the war and the human problem for good. The research was extraordinarily dangerous, so military command dared not locate it on any of the inhabited Tollean worlds for fear of political repercussions.

The compromise was to put it somewhere an accident would do minimum harm, and not be noticed. Inevitably, this world, not far from the newest and biggest Tollean base in this sector, was chosen.

The research was an outside chance at best, and Command did not intend to waste its finest military men on something that might never produce a usable return. A contingent of officers and men considered dispensable would support and protect the scientists. The word 'dispensable' made Koll livid.

The order to return here came as a complete shock. Koll's career had gone well until the fateful day he insulted and upset a superior officer. A momentary loss of control, a moment when the difference between the way he was treated and the way he thought he ought to be, blossomed into an indiscretion destined to limit his prospects forever.

An unexpected promotion came the next week, followed by assignment to the position of coordinator in the most out-of-the-way hole in the galaxy. Forced to leave his wife and children—he would never expose them to a hellish place like this—he was now nursemaid to the researchers.

There was no glory here, and no future. It was clear he had been deliberately promoted into oblivion, and would remain there unless he could find a way to escape. With luck, those fools of scientists in his charge would complete their work quickly so he could get back to the war and a better posting.

On arrival, Koll ordered the disposal of the human bodies left here three years ago. There would be little remaining, but for reasons of morale, if nothing else, it still needed dealing with, at least from the compound area.

Skeletons filled the underground workings, but other areas were strangely clear, in this town at least. Here and there, scorch marks from fires told the story, the ash now washed away by the oftentimes heavy rains of this planet.

At some stage, a human ship must have snuck through to check the settlements, and burnt many of the bodies in this one. Considering he had cleared the planet three years ago, it was the only possible explanation.

Nothing similar had taken place at the other settlements, where bones lay everywhere, scattered by the local wildlife and the weather. Koll had visited them first, settling on this site because of the proximity of the mine compound and spaceport. Located in a coastal valley cutting back into the steep mountains, this one was also more sheltered and less damaged.

Disgusted with the situation, he climbed back into the cabin of his landing craft. Once sealed, insulated, and fitted with an air filtration and cooling plant, the old mine office would be his new quarters. He did not intend to set foot outside his shuttle again until it was ready.

***

On a ledge high on the hillside, Echo lay on her belly and watched the activity. After years of praying a ship would come, the only arrivals sat on the airfield below, and they belonged to the Tolleani.

After grabbing her emergency pack and heading for the surrounding forest, she had made her way to the ledge to see what was happening. Far below, the original shuttle sat on the tarmac with a distinct air of permanency. Several others had come, disgorged equipment and supplies, and left.

Now another ship had landed, a type Echo had never seen before, but clearly military. Its dark-gray, sinister shape squatted like a giant bug at the far side of the field, just meters away from the airfield offices and barracks. The monsters were here to stay.

The town was no longer safe, so she would have to leave. The possibility that something like this might occur had haunted her for years, but she was prepared. Her father's prospecting hut, hidden away in the mountain gorges, would become her refuge. After the massacre, she had prepared the old cabin for just such an emergency, and now it would serve as home until the aliens went away again.

***

Another year on.

Field-General Bradford Molliner adjusted his eyeglasses and studied the paper. A worst-case scenario had now become a distinct possibility. With supplies of Trilatenite critical, the high command was now ordering him to do something to fix it.

His jurisdiction included Corros, one of only three human planets with significant deposits of the mineral, but the settlements on that world had been wiped out by alien attack years ago. The war front now sat between here, the major sector base on Cymbel 3, and that distant world.

He sighed, leaned across the desk, and tapped the intercom.

"Heather, can you ask Marshal Bentleigh to come in here, please?" A brief acknowledgement sounded on the speaker.

No ship had approached Corros for years. Soon after the initial attack on the world, several ore carriers had disappeared without a trace, and a hold on further voyages was instigated.

A stealth drone sent into the system found the orbiting navigation satellites of Corros destroyed, and Tollean activity was detected near a wormhole in the system. The drone turned tail and ran home, sounding the alarm.

Months later, a military scout was sent to examine the colonies from orbit. They found only destruction, ashes, and bodies, with no traces of human life. Limited by their position behind enemy lines, they left without landing.

Now, Molliner realized, he would have to send another to determine whether retaking the planet was a possibility. He had the perfect vessel for the task, a new experimental model designed for behind-the-lines missions. With the ability to sneak unseen past the battlefront, it could carry out a quick, quiet examination of the mine sites. A positive report was a precursor to a major military push to take back and protect Corros.

His bigger problem involved whom to send. Top-quality captains were hard to come by and could not be spared for surveillance missions, the exact reason why the stealth ship remained unused on the tarmac just a few hundred meters from his window.

Someone needed to be promoted. One young officer, Ben Teague, was ready, and he was Molliner's first choice, but politics was now the deciding factor.

The son of the Viceroy, Ballinor Clarke, was also overdue for his commander's bars, and the planetary leader had made it quite clear he expected his lackluster offspring to receive the next ship off the blocks.

By the time Bentleigh arrived, Molliner had reached a decision; Clarke would command the mission with Teague as his second, as a precaution.

***

"Thirty seconds, Captain."

Ben Teague took a deep breath and focused on his monitors. Four sets of eyes awaited the appearance of the last of the planet's mining communities, focusing on the long line of jagged stone teeth as a high, saw-tooth ridge drew nearer on the screens.

Earlier flyovers of the other towns had detected no trace of human life: when the Tolleani invaded a world, they left no survivors. The infrastructure and mine workings, on the other hand, were largely undamaged, so re-commissioning would be a simple matter. Only the supporting naval base had suffered extensive damage.

"Any minute now," Captain Gordon Clarke warned.

Ben's fingers waltzed across the controls as the vessel crested the rise and began a descent towards the small airstrip on the valley floor ahead. "No ships down there. No sign of movement."

"Fine. Do a sweep of the mine and the town—"

Without warning, the screens flickered, lights in the cabin dimmed, and from outside the hull shell the whine of the engines faded as they powered down.

"Commence emergency landing procedures. Set her down on manual. Now, please." The captain's voice remained calm, as if events like this occurred every day.

Turning the ship into a powerless glide over the airfield, Ben hit the landing gear switch and battled to align the vessel for what promised to be a rough and dangerous descent. The crew had no time to brace as the ship slammed onto the field with a bone-shaking thud, careening across the hard-packed surface towards the largest of the spaceport's Quonset hangars. The ear-splitting scream of steel skids on gravel rent the air, sparks streaming behind as the craft slowed and ground to a halt meters from the refueling bowsers.

Ben gasped and slumped back in his seat. "That was fun. What in the hells happened?"

"That's what we need to find out," the captain said. "What's our status?"

"Life-support and emergency backups are optimal. Internal systems are still functioning."

"Run a complete check, please."

"Some minor systems are out, but we can reset them. That's not our main problem."

"And that would be…?"

Ben diverted the primary engine readouts to the captain's monitor. "Activating circuits in the engine pods have shut down, Sir. All at the same time."

"Impossible. Those things are hardened against damage."

"Yeah … never happened before. We can't reset them without going outside, and it'll take at least forty minutes for one person, less if two of us go."

"Are the security systems functional?"

"Yes, Sir."

"Turn them on now. Nobody goes out until we are sure this place is safe."

An hour later, the airstrip still appeared deserted. Dust swirling across the ground was the only movement, the only sound the hollow whistle of wind blowing down from the mountains.

"There's nothing out there, captain," a female voice reported from further aft in the cabin. "No disturbances and no infra-red anywhere near us."

"Makes no sense," Clarke said. "If this is an attack, someone is responsible. What about the buildings?"

"Most of them are heat-insulated, so anyone inside won't show on the detectors."

"What do you think, Second?"

"Not sure," Ben replied. "Other than introduced stock species, we haven't detected any non-indigenous life here, human or Tollean. Our problem might just be faulty relays. If one activator went when the failure occurred, the others might go from the overload. I mean, this is a new, unproven ship."

"And it's been thoroughly tested. Activator failure is not supposed to happen."

"No, Sir. Only speculating … Sir."

The captain rubbed his chin. "Okay, the engines first. Someone has to go outside regardless, to reset and check the damned circuits; otherwise we won't be leaving anytime soon. The quicker we deal with it, the sooner we'll be away; already been here too long. Two on the circuits, two on guard. Now!"

"Sir?" Ben threw an incredulous glance at his superior officer. It was a bad call. Leaving the bridge unmanned was well outside standard procedure.

"That's an order, Second."

This was the captain's first ship, Ben knew, granted through political pressure rather than innate ability. Molliner had cautioned him about Clarke before the mission and advised him of the reason why he was placed second in command. However, a dubious order on a deserted airfield was not grounds for dissension. Ben doubted the wisdom of the decision but kept his peace.

I should remain inside, he thought.

The tarmac was hot, dusty, and deserted. Ben reached up into the open panel on the port engine pod and finished resetting the switches on the engine activator. Just across from him, Jack Rayne, the navigator, did likewise to the starboard engine.

It had taken only fifteen minutes to re-calibrate the units, and the reset was the last thing to be done. Ben closed the panel and secured it before turning back to the ship's main hatch.

Not far away, Captain Clarke stood gazing across towards the administration buildings, a laser rifle held casually in his hands. On the far side of the vessel, Jill Riley, the ship's communications officer, likewise stood guard, her attention a little more focused than the Captain's.

Reaching up to the hull shell beside the boarding ladder, Ben opened the external access control panel to check that the ship's security systems were still functioning properly. Suddenly, Jill let out a yell.

Beneath the hull, Ben saw figures rising over the top of the earthworks that ran between the airfield and the stream that ran along one side. Six Tollean soldiers stepped up and fired at the ground beside the ship.

At the same time, a second group of soldiers stepped up to the far edge of the field from a large storage pond adjacent to the mine, and yet more emerged from the nearby Quonset hangar. All were heavily armed, but no more shots were fired.

The aliens advanced slowly, weapons raised and ready. Ben reached up and slammed a hand against the emergency security-set button, then stood back, waiting. Above him, the hatch closed and the ladder withdrew into the hull.

The aliens clearly did not want to kill him and his crew. They no doubt intended to take the ship, but Ben's action would make that an extremely difficult proposition.

For minutes, nobody moved. None of the other crew could reach the ship without being shot, and there appeared to be no apparent value in their returning fire. At least fifteen Tolleani surrounded them, and one, an officer, was walking slowly forward. Stopping several meters from Clarke, he made a motion for the captain to drop his weapon.

Shoot the bastard, Ben thought.

Clarke dropped his rifle to the ground and slowly raised his hands in surrender. Unwilling to become the sacrifice, Jill Riley did the same.

Chapter Five

"SO, WHAT HAVE YOU done with my rescuers, you bastards?" Echo lay on her belly at the edge of the rocky outcrop, peered down through the early morning mist, and cursed the sweat as it beaded on her skin and trickled into all the wrong places. Of all things in this world, she hated the heat and humidity the most.

At least it kept the monsters indoors, she thought. Good for me.

Rolling over to relieve the irritation from a sharp rock digging into her groin, she gazed out towards the distant ocean. As usual, rain had fallen during the night. With the storm gone, the hot morning sun streamed through the clouds in long curtains, boiling away the morning mist that lay like a thin blanket over the valley.

Still shrouded by the remnant haze, the blocky, indistinct shapes of the old, now forsaken town shimmered in the near distance. Echo remembered her childhood there with fondness: the wondrous life of a teenager, the days filled with a firm conviction of the infallibility of her own place in life.

No longer.

Far below, a cluster of prefabricated timber and fibro buildings marked the old mine administration precinct. Next to the compound, the adjacent airfield emerged through the mist. Where once ore carriers and supply vessels landed, two deadly-looking alien craft now stood. A pair of smaller atmospheric scout cars, intended for general surveillance, squatted nearby like giant bugs. Echo never saw the aircrews; they spent their days in the barracks, venturing outside as little as possible. The aliens hated the environment of this planet.

A new arrival, sleek and black, sat at the front of one of the hangers. Unmistakably human in origin and branded with the roundel of the Federation Fleet, it had appeared several weeks earlier. Echo had not witnessed the arrival but came more often now, hoping to spot the crew. It puzzled her as to why they landed here, in enemy-occupied territory. She wondered if they had come to rescue her.

For years, she had prayed for an end to her involuntary solitude. From her hidden refuge in the forest, she waited, watched, and listened for the telltale signs and sounds of a human ship. Other than the new one on the airstrip, none had ever come. This one was not showing much promise.

Confident of eventual rescue, she had kept her head down and survived. Only on rare occasions did she consider whether she might die on this world, but recently the possibility had begun to loom larger in her mind.

This outcrop was the same from which she watched the return of the aliens a year earlier. She visited here regularly to spy on the camp.

Movement caught her eye as a small group emerged from a building and made its way through the center of the compound. Four human figures dressed in pale blue coveralls were visible, walking under armed escort.

"God's halls, you're still alive." Echo gasped. This was unexpected. Perhaps there was hope yet.

As the small assembly reached its destination, the lead guard singled out a prisoner and marched him behind the nearby buildings. Within minutes, an alarm sounded, sending more guards rushing from the barracks.

From Echo's position, parts of the complex were hidden from view, but everything pointed towards the prisoner having attempted an escape. Harsh, guttural shouts drifted up from below, followed by the signature flash of laser fire from beyond the outermost buildings, and then calm.

After a drawn-out interval, the tall figure she had long ago identified as the alien commandant stepped from the old mine office and strolled towards the rear of the camp, reappearing minutes later in the company of two guards. Leaving them at attention on the concourse, he returned to his sanctuary. The other prisoners were gone, long since taken into one of the buildings.

One down, Echo thought. The escapee was dead. As the base settled back to its normal, routine slumber, the remaining soldiers retreated to their quarters. Other than the two unfortunates standing for punishment in the hot morning sun, the place soon looked deserted once again.

Echo knew better. The aliens hardly ever showed themselves, but from past observation, she knew how many there were and where they would be at any given time.

She often watched the Tolleani. From a distance, they appeared humanoid, apart from the head, hands and feet, but larger and uglier. Waiting for rescue was a lonely occupation, and with no one else in her life, these creatures had become the major focus for her curiosity and a constant source of fascination.

Apparently all male, they were not unlike humans. She wondered about them often: what their females were like, whether they had families at all, how they reproduced, what they did for amusement, or if they even understood the term.

Careful to remain unseen, Echo wriggled back from the edge of the rocks, lifted into a crouch, and crept into the undergrowth. She cursed under her breath.

"Murdering bastards!"

***

"So … Leaving again, are we?" Barbus Koll dropped the binoculars to his lap and gazed out the grimy window of his office at the rocky outcrop on the hillside.

He had first discovered the human's presence from the light reflected by an ocular device similar to his own. For months, he had watched the creature come and go, believing itself to be invisible.

Its frequent appearances had proven a minor source of amusement over time, and a welcome break from the boring tedium. No doubt a survivor from the earlier cleanup operation, it must now be hiding somewhere in the mountains behind the mine.

It posed no threat to him or his command. Worth neither catching nor killing, its apprehension would be a waste of precious resources. In the future, if his superiors ever gave him more than the handful of useless rejects he now commanded, he might find the time.

From previous dealings, Koll knew humans to be troublesome. When Tollean Command first began exterminating them, they hit back hard and effectively. By his standards, these animals were less than civilized and did not warrant any kind of special consideration. He acknowledged the fact without reservation.

Despite their technology, they were no different from any other dangerous animal: a powerful bite, but still not worth the effort. This one appeared every few days, watched the base for a while, and then departed. Other than occasionally sneaking around the town and the overgrown fields, it never did anything to concern him.

In the last year, he had learned to loath this damned planet even more than before. Apart from the unholy heat, every insect on this pathetic rock wanted to sting him, and every animal went into frenzy at his approach. Every plant stung, burned, or poisoned, and nothing here was edible. Each scrap of food had to be imported. The humidity gave him an irritating rash. Koll thanked the ancestors the atmosphere was breathable, even if it did stink. At least the air in this building was conditioned.

In the last year, he had discovered a little more about the secret research he protected. The three scientists treated him like hired help and told him nothing, but he kept them under close surveillance and listened in to their conversations. Their laboratory, private quarters, and the machine shop they had set up in the old mine workshops were all thoroughly wired. In his opinion, nothing on this base should be beyond his jurisdiction.

One of their projects, the one warranting exile to this world, was an explosive apparatus of some kind. The device, they claimed, would trigger an atmospheric chain reaction, wiping all life from the surface of a planet to leave it clean and ready for the reforming crews. Atmosphere could be easily replaced, an empty world quickly transformed into a site more suitable for the Tolleani.

Given the choice, Koll thought he would rather be as far from here as possible and to hell with the scientists. Tired and bored, he closed his eyes, letting his mind wander.

If those idiot researchers ever succeeded, humans would cease to be a problem. The war would be done, and he would be an over commander. Human planets would fall in a single sweep, with this place the first he would destroy. The Empire only had a use for the minerals, not the wildlife or those annoying humans. Meanwhile, it was still too hot here for his liking. Deep in contemplation, he swiveled back towards the desk.

A new problem had just arisen. A few weeks ago, his tame scientists used one of their new toys to capture an enemy warship. A Terran ship had been detected entering orbit around the planet, and the scientists insisted they could use it to test one of their new creations. The device was beyond his understanding, but he had no interest in how it worked; only in what it could do.

With just enough time to set a trap, Koll moved the ships on the airfield into the hangars and got his men out of sight. Unaware of the Tolleani presence, the Terran spacecraft lost power whilst cresting the nearby ridge, managing to make a very skillful emergency landing on the airstrip. The crew had been his prisoners since then.

Koll sighed again. Minutes earlier, one of them had killed a guard and escaped, diving into the water-filled depression behind the compound. The sentries failed to stop the creature with small arms fire. It emerged from the pond and vanished into the forest long before they could reach it around the perimeter.

To Koll, the situation was a minor irritation. With no more inclination to send men looking for an absconder than to search for the human survivor, his main concern was why the escape had occurred at all. The fault was his for sending only one guard to do a job when he should have sent several, but nothing about that would ever appear in an official report.

He wanted the alien ship undamaged, but the hull was highly energized, a simple but effective way to defeat his best efforts at gaining entry. The obvious solution was to force one of the prisoners to deactivate it on pain of death, but the creature had attacked its escort and fled.

Koll made a mental note. These creatures were not as helpless as he expected. Two guards per human from now on. With any luck, the escapee would die in the mountains, but if it somehow survived, a search party might become necessary. Humans were fragile, but the other one had managed to survive in the wilderness, so this one might as well. One itch could be ignored, but not two.

Leaning back in his chair, he took a deep breath of the sweet, filtered air in the office, dreaming of the day his assignment would end and of his victorious return to the center of the Empire. The research would end the war. Leaving this accursed place would be bliss, and the return to the Tollean home world a triumph. Dinners, honors, appearances … wealth?

Chapter Six

BEN SLIPPED ON THE damp, rotting morass beneath his feet then tumbled and crashed through the undergrowth, coming to a grinding halt face down at the base of a steep gully with something sharp poking him in the groin.

Scrambling from the mound of flattened vegetation that broke his fall, he brushed himself off, subconsciously wiping blood from the scratches on his face and hands.

This was not going well. Only two days since escaping, and he was lost. These ridges divided an impenetrable maze of narrow gorges, every one filled with choking plant life, each requiring a seeming eternity to navigate. For a man who had spent most of his life in space, it was the nearest thing to the hells he had ever experienced. A Tollean cage did not seem so bad now, and he wondered why he had bothered to escape at all.

On something resembling an old, rotting log, he sat and tried to reorient himself. Rain had fallen in the night, but beneath the dense canopy, the drops never reached the ground, filtering down instead as a fine, diffuse mist. Moisture from the dank air settled on his face and soaked into his now tattered uniform.

Sheer walls ran along both sides of this canyon, tangled jungle filling the almost-level floor between. The trees stretched at least twenty meters above Ben's head and almost blocked out the sunlight.

A strong, musty odor drifted from the thick carpet of multi-hued moss to assail Ben's nostrils, and each color of the mossy rainbow made its own small assertion in the dim light of the under-story. Nearby, something unseen rustled in the bracken, moving away from his intrusion.

The native fauna did not concern him. Before the mission, he and the other members of the crew had received a full briefing on this world. Ninety-five percent Terran in nature and more hospitable than modern-day Old Earth, according to the official line, Corros possessed few dangerous indigenous life forms. While not totally incompatible, the native biology was sufficiently so that most of the micro-organisms were also harmless to humans.

Animal attack was not a problem, but survival was. Ben needed water desperately, or he would never have attempted the recent descent into the canyon. The dampness from his face and clothes served to keep his mouth moist but he needed more.

Somewhere through the undergrowth, a stream tinkled. After a deep breath of the cool, damp forest air, Ben climbed to his aching feet and stumbled towards the sound.

Not far away, a mountain creek flowed along the floor of the canyon, clear, fresh water tumbling in rills and pools over the bare, sun-washed rocks. The path cut through the jungle by the watercourse offered the first open passage Ben had encountered all day.

After a much-needed drink from a small waterfall, he turned and picked his way along the bank, heading downstream. Betrayed long ago by a less-than-optimum sense of direction, he prayed the creek would lead back towards the mining camp, or at least to the nearby coast.

After two days lost, the only hope lay in returning to the ship. The rest of the crew were still prisoners, and beyond his survival, their rescue was priority number one. He would not free them by dying here. Duty! Duty, always first. An acceptable plan could wait until he was out of this mess.

Clothes wet from the rain and mist, he sat on the rocky bank to recuperate, the sun's warmth a welcome change from the dark and damp of the forest. Rested but content to sit for a moment longer, he cast a wary eye towards the opposite tree line.

On the far side of the stream, visibility beneath the trees extended almost as far back as the cliff base. The vegetation opened up a little there, the canopy extending right to the water's edge, but the under-story clearer. The ubiquitous moss looked well-worn in places, probably from the passage of animals. Further back in the dim light at the edge of sight, the open area gave way to a mass of tangled vines.

And a solitary window.

Hidden in the shadows was a structure, most likely built long ago by the first colonists. Startled by the unexpected sight, Ben picked his way across the rocks and crept up the bank.

A cabin materialized in the gloom. One end of a narrow veranda with a closed door and a window was visible, the remainder covered by a cascade of forest lianas that flowed across the roof and down in a curtain at the front. Old, worn, and derelict, it was nevertheless intact. The walls stood strong, the weathered planks well secured. The window frame still contained glass, and the door had a new hinge.

Someone maintained this place, Ben realized.

He crept up to the porch. Motionless, he listened for sounds of movement from within and then, satisfied he was alone, eased the door open. The interior was dim, but as his eyes adjusted to the shadows, a single room revealed itself, about six meters square and as rough as the exterior. It was clean and tidy.

Someone lives here.

Just inside the door, two wooden chairs stood by an old table. Still exhausted, Ben sat and looked around. Urged on by the persistent snarl from an empty stomach, his first instinct was to look for something, anything, edible.

On a crude bench against the side wall sat a jumbled assortment of fruits and vegetables. *Terran*, he thought. *The Tolleani can't tolerate this stuff.* It was mildly toxic to their biology, so they would not store it here. And it was fresh, more or less.

A tin of salted meat, labeled with a Cymbelian manufacturer's tag and apparently still edible, sat near the other items and immediately drew Ben's eye. Satisfied the occupant of the cabin was human, Ben lunged at the bench, hauled the newfound treasure to the table, and began an assault on the tin.

The rest of the room contained very few furnishings. A stack of boxes stood at the back beside an ancient, cast-iron, wood-burning stove and a pile of cut and stacked firewood. A mug containing two old and well-worn toothbrushes sat on the table, and a double mattress lay by the back wall.

You don't sleep there, do you, Ben decided. Hidden in the darkest corner behind the door was a small cot. Smart. Stay where you won't be seen by someone coming in unannounced.

The canned meat gone, Ben moved a chair and sat by the window, eyes on the stream outside. He toyed aimlessly with one of the toothbrushes, wondering if two people were living here. Nobody was around, but Ben suspected the occupant would return eventually.

Alert for outside sounds, he chewed on what remained of the raw vegetables, his first rations in days. No doubt, the owner would be upset with the food theft, but ignorance of which native plants were safe made living off the land risky, and hunger was an urge difficult to resist.

He wondered if this might be the refuge of a survivor from the mining town. That seemed unlikely; the colonies were declared dead years ago. On the other hand, there was no other possible explanation.

Given the state of the war, no attempts had been made to recolonize this world until now. Ben's mission was strategic, and the team's orders to determine if the mines were recoverable did not involve looking for survivors. Central Command long ago discounted the possibility of anyone surviving alone out here. *Guess they're wrong*, Ben thought.

Exhausted from his battle with the forest, his eyelids began to droop, prompting a move to the cot. He would wait, hidden behind the door, until the occupant of the shack returned. Exhausted, he never knew when consciousness succumbed to a deep sleep.

***

Echo squatted in the tangled undergrowth at the edge of the deserted fields, watching the gardens of the old town. At first glance, they resembled any wild meadow. Years of inattention had allowed the crops to self-seed and survive, but in most places, local flora now spread unhindered through the gardens. Native life on Corros competed poorly with the stronger, engineered Terran species, and useful food plants still grew among the weeds. It was the only reason she ever came here.

The monsters never entered the old gardens. Untended, and not pruned for years, the fruit trees still yielded small harvests of suspect quality fruit, mostly edible and little touched by native insect pests. Nothing moved in the garden area other than the odd, grazing pig or goat, now wild after years of freedom.

Beyond the fence line, Echo found a decent scavenging patch. Taking only what she needed, she covered the scars of her digging to minimize the chances of discovery. The Tolleani did not know she foraged here, and the longer they stayed ignorant, the better.

A week ago, she found tomato plants, but now they were gone, most likely cut to the ground by grazing animals. There had been a lot of that in the last few weeks. Root vegetables were still find-able: apart from pigs, the animals tended not to dig too deep.

With a full satchel, she returned to the edge of the field and looked across to the town. Her old home was the nearest building.

Bad memories.

Shaking her head, she turned away.

There would be no trip into the town today.

On the animal path leading back into the mountains, Echo paused as a small, wild piglet crossed the track to forage in the undergrowth opposite. Minutes later, it moved away. A juicy pork roast would have been a real treat, but not this time. The adult pigs were somewhere nearby.

It was always safer to avoid these creatures. Some of them, the males in particular, were now far too dangerous to approach, growing larger and more aggressive each year. Engineered for this world, they thrived on the native vegetation.

A survivalist at heart, her father had instructed her in hunting and subsistence in the wild. She had managed to remain fit and healthy and had coped well on a mixture of terrestrial and native plants and animals despite a few minor bouts of gastric poisoning. She knew what vegetation was edible without repercussions and what should be avoided.

Most of the native fare she left alone. At best, it produced a disquieting heaviness in the gut, and at worst, made her vomit and dry retch for hours on end. Only one plant, a spinach-like green growing along the watercourses, was a regular source of sustenance, but she often had to fight the pigs for it. Releasing them had been a mistake.

As she walked, Echo's thoughts turned to rescue, as it often did. Her rescuers had been captured, and she wondered if another ship would ever come. She accepted the inevitable fact that until that happened, or the aliens captured or killed her, death from starvation remained a distinct possibility. The town gardens were failing, and food was getting scarcer.

Deeper still was her wish for the simple touch of another human being, someone she could talk to. Since the attack, she had often wished for companionship. Anyone would do—anyone at all. The chances grew dimmer with each passing day.

Perhaps I'll die from loneliness first.

Most of the long, arduous journey home followed old, well-worn wildlife trails. Deeper in the forest now, she scrambled down-slope through the trees to a fast-flowing stream and waded through the shallows, moving higher into the mountain canyons.

The old prospecting hut was still solid despite its extreme age and provided a perfect refuge hidden from view to all but the closest and most observant eyes. Dense, tangled vegetation almost covered the structure, and with all the access paths overgrown, it was invisible from the air and approachable only from the stream. She drew closer and then hesitated. Something was wrong here.

Attuned to the environment by years of solitude, Echo sensed a presence. Her forehead creased by a deep frown, she knelt on the grass and reached over a shoulder for the hunting crossbow she always carried on her back.

Confidence wavering, she fitted a bolt to the bow and crept forward, certain the monsters had finally found her. The cabin door was slightly ajar.

She always closed it.

Easing it open, she peered inside. Her eyes still adjusting from the brighter daylight outside, little was visible in the dim interior. Silence filled the room.

Behind the door, she thought. *That's where I would be.*

Stepping forward, she dropped the satchel to the floor and swung around to face the front of the room. With the weapon raised, she peered into the darkest corner.

A shadow moved.

Echo froze.

Her breath caught as she fought to keep her hands steady. No one had ever intruded into this place before. The trespasser was human, dressed in a dirty, battered, pale-blue uniform. Visible on his clothing was a symbol identical to the roundel on the spacecraft at the airstrip. A loud snore broke the silence.

As her eyes adjusted to the dim light, she moved forward. She had not seen another person for years, and now a stranger lay on her bed.

Gods, a man. Deep inside, Echo was overjoyed to see anybody human, but from his uniform, this was a pilot, someone who could fly her off this forsaken planet. He was attractive despite the dirt and blood. A bit stinky though, she thought. The odor was familiar, something not smelled for years, the aroma of sweat—masculine sweat. Deep inside, her stomach twisted with a shiver of excitement tinged with fear. Besides her father and brother, the only males she had ever known well were the boys at school.

Mesmerized by the intruder's presence, she edged closer, unable to help herself despite an acute sense of caution. Reaching out with one foot, she poked him in the side. With a sudden jerk, he sat up and looked for his attacker.

Echo heard the pulse pounding in her ears. "Don't move." Trembling from head to toe, she pushed her crossbow forward, fighting to hold the business end steady. "You're one of the crew. I mean … from the ship that arrived a few weeks ago."

Ben wiped the sleep from his eyes and peered at the figure standing over him, a young woman dressed in old, tattered cargo shorts and a dirty, checked shirt rolled up at the sleeves.

"This is a dream, right?" Rubbing his eyes again, he swung his legs off the cot. As he stood, his eyes locked onto what appeared to be a medieval crossbow pointed at his stomach.

"You escaped the day before yesterday," Echo said. "I saw you. I thought the monsters killed you."

"I'm hard to kill. Can you put that thing away? I'm not dangerous. I don't mean you any harm. I'm a friend, human, like you."

For what seemed an eternity to Ben, Echo remained motionless, then lowered the bow to point at the floor. Edging across to a wall, she hung the weapon on a hook and turned back towards him, running a hand through her light-brown hair in an attempt to tidy her tangled, waist-length ponytail.

The immediate threat reduced, Ben examined his assailant. The girl was tall but several inches shorter than he, and fit, her figure trim and athletic. From her skin color and facial features, she was of Terran-Caucasian heritage. Large, green, almond eyes framed in a small, heart-shaped face glared at him as if he were some kind of insect. The grim, determined set of her mouth warned she was not to be interfered with.

Ben sighed and stretched himself. The girl was not so dangerous, he decided, and was cute in a rough kind of way. Beneath the grime and the rat's nest of hair, she seemed quite attractive, and the last thing he expected to find on this world. "I'm sorry," he said. "I didn't mean to startle you."

Echo gestured towards the scraps on the nearby table. "You ate my food."

"Mm … Yeah, sorry. I'm starving. Is there any more?"

Chapter Seven

ECHO BACKED AWAY AND sat at the table to remove her old, battered miner's boots. Still trembling inside, she studied the intruder.

On first impression, he did not appear a threat, but she kept her eyes glued to him regardless as he moved across to sit down opposite her. Not that he frightened her—nothing did, except the aliens—but he was the first human she had seen in four years.

Beneath his grimy flight uniform, he was tall, strong, and undeniably attractive, with brown hair and tanned skin. His blue eyes betrayed complete exhaustion as he ran battered fingertips across several weeks of beard growth and then the dark, bloody scratches on his hands. Unarmed, he appeared harmless, so Echo decided to take a risk and trust him, for now.

Leaning forward, she grabbed the satchel from the floor. Several fresh fruits and vegetables rolled onto the table. "These can be eaten raw," she said. "The stove can't be lit until after dark, otherwise the monsters will spot the smoke. Don't worry; I washed them in the stream."

"Monsters? The Tolleani?"

"Yes, them."

"Oh, okay. Bastards, certainly. I don't know if I would classify them as monsters. They're quite advanced, really, more than us in some ways. Don't think like us though. No empathy."

"I hate them."

"Yeah, I suppose you would, considering." Ben gnawed at a raw turnip, running his eyes over the other items Echo had provided. "This is good. My last decent meal was a week ago."

"You ate my tin of meat. You're lucky."

"Yeah, sorry. Why am I lucky?"

"You're still alive. That tin was four years old. What have you been eating since they caught you?"

"Same as this—anything they thought we might eat from the old town gardens. Mostly rubbish. Got some good tomatoes a week back."

"My tomatoes…"

Ben leaned back in the unstable chair and studied the unlikely individual seated opposite. At the time of the attack, she must have been a child, a teenager now grown into a beautiful young woman.

"What in the Gods' halls are you doing here? My reports say the Tolleani wiped out this colony."

"I wasn't in the town when they attacked. I hid in the forest, and the monsters never found me."

"You survived all this time in these mountains?"

"No." Echo squirmed in her seat, self-conscious beneath his scrutiny. "I went home after they left. They came back, so I moved here."

"And they never come after you?"

"They don't know I'm here."

Ben looked down at the tabletop. "I doubt that." He wondered how she had coped, surviving alone in the wild surrounded by the remnants of her lost life. Unconfirmed—and obviously wrong—reports said the enemy had killed everyone following their normal convention. Ergo, this girl should not be alive.

Echo sat in silence as her visitor ate. Unable to help herself, she fixated on his every movement. Still a little wary, she accepted that he did not pose a threat. After all, they were in the same situation.

Perhaps in his early thirties, he was older by ten years or more. Despite her best efforts, she could not drag her eyes away. Notwithstanding his current state of disrepair, she found him mesmerizing.

Despite being covered in scratches and grime and looking like the survivor of an animal attack, he spoke with confidence and self-assurance, not at all perturbed by the strangeness of the situation in which he now found himself. He behaved as if he had been here for years.

"Who are you?"

He barely paused from eating. "Ben Teague. You?"

"Oh. Echo—Echo Bourke. Did you come here to rescue me?"

"Sorry, no. We didn't expect survivors here. The Tolleani never leave…" For a moment, he paused. "Why 'Echo'?"

"My dad's pet name for me. He's dead now. He used to say I always bounce back, like an echo. My real name's Cinta, but no one ever calls … called me that."

A frown furrowed her brow as she spoke, fingers fidgeting, never stopping for more than a few seconds as they tapped out an irregular drumbeat on the tabletop. Those deep, piercing eyes had not left Ben since his rude awakening.

"Don't worry. I won't hurt you. I'm quite harmless."

Echo sat back and sighed, but still did not divert her gaze.

"How do I reach the airstrip from here?" Ben asked. "Can you tell me an easy way?"

The question startled Echo, dragging her back from the fringes of her imagination. "What, now?"

"No, soon. Sleep first and then go back to my ship. Those bastards disabled it somehow and forced us down; I need to know how they did it."

"What happened?"

"We flew over the other towns and the air base, but they were deserted—wiped out. We expected the same here, but when we arrived, the drive systems cut out without warning, forcing us to land at the mine. Something disabled critical circuits in the ship's engines. I think they have a new weapon, something never seen before."

"What about the monsters? Didn't you spot them before you landed?"

"No, the place looked deserted. No ships, no aliens, nothing. We waited for an hour before stepping out to check the engines. I was about to go back on board when the Tolleani appeared all around us. It was a well-prepared trap; they expected us."

"Why would you… I mean, you can't go back now. You only just escaped." Overwhelmed by the sudden appearance of another human being, she had never considered that he might not stay. "It's unsafe. They'll kill you."

"No choice: I'm a Fleet officer. I must find out how those bastards grounded us, destroy whatever they used, get my ship back, and rescue my crew. They're still prisoners. And I need to report this outpost."

"They'll kill you." Tears welled in Echo's eyes. After years of waiting, someone had come for her at last, and all he wanted to do was leave again. If he died, so did her chance of escape.

"I'll avoid that if I can," he replied. "Can't sit here and do nothing. Got to try, at least."

At that moment, Echo realized he would not be dissuaded. To a military officer and a spacer, duty always came first. "Can I … you … you'll take me with you when you go?"

"Yes, of course. After I have my ship and crew back, we'll pick you up. Can't leave you on your own. I doubt you would survive here much longer."

"I am not helpless, thank you." Echo blushed, incensed by his assumption. "I'm perfectly capable of surviving alone." She knew it was not true: survival was becoming harder every day. She did not want to stay any longer. Not now.

"I'm sure you are, but I'm still a fleet officer. I have a duty, and you are now part of that, regardless."

Echo's brow wrinkled. That this stranger should decide to make her his responsibility annoyed her a little, but equally, she felt happy that someone, anyone, should care. At this moment, she needed that more than anything else.

"Fine, I'll show you the way down tomorrow morning. You do know they'll catch you again, don't you?"

"Not if I'm careful. If I can get to my ship undiscovered, I can get my laser pistols. Any weapons here?"

"Only my crossbow. Oh, and some old kitchen knives." Echo pointed to a battered carton on the floor by the stove.

"No guns?"

"I had some once, but the batteries went flat. Can't recharge them here."

Ben rifled through the contents of the box, tested the sharpness of each item, and extracted a heavy, wood-handled carving knife. Delving further, he also removed a short, still sharp, paring blade.

"This'll do," he said. "Um, where do you wash around here? You know, clothes, bath?"

Echo's face flushed as she realized how disheveled she must appear. "I don't worry too much on my own. Nobody to…"

"No, me. I want to get the mud out of my clothes, and I'm a mess. Haven't shaved since they caught me a couple of weeks ago. I need to scrub up."

"Oh, you can use the stream. The pool out in front is good. You can dry your things on those flat rocks. The sun won't go down for hours."

"Soap?"

"No, sand."

Ben stopped as he neared the door. "Is the water safe? Any nasties?"

"No, its fine. Nothing here can hurt you unless you eat it. No dangerous animals except wild pigs, and the bugs don't like us. I guess we smell bad to them." She regretted her words immediately.

Ben grinned as he exited the cabin and headed in the direction indicated. Echo sat motionless at the table, her heart thumping and her skin hot with anger and embarrassment.

Nice one, girl, she thought. Screw it up, why don't you. First man to come along in four years, and you look like a shit-heap on legs.

Half an hour later, her self-discipline somewhat restored, Echo stood and peeked through the doorway. Drawn by the sounds of splashing, she crept outside. At the center of the stream, Ben sat on the rocks, his washed coveralls spread out beside him.

Reasonably sure that it was unacceptable to be watching, Echo crouched behind the bushes. In the back of her mind, a faint voice scolded her that it was wrong to invade the man's privacy, but she could not help herself.

Never before had she seen anyone like him. With his back to her and oblivious to her presence, he gazed towards the creek bank opposite. Close to two meters tall and well muscled, his body glistened with wetness. In the light of late afternoon, his skin glowed with a golden bronze tan. Not an ounce of fat betrayed the precision, each muscle cleanly defined beneath smooth skin.

Echo's eyes lingered on his short, brown hair. A dark line of tattooed characters ran down his right flank from below the armpit to the hip. Never before had she seen anything like that. It appeared to be letters, but in a language she did not understand. He stood motionless, running fingers through his wet hair as he gazed downstream. Echo ducked lower as he turned to attend to his clothing.

She wondered if she was just a 'responsibility' for him. Older and obviously more experienced, he undoubtedly saw her as a child, and appeared much too preoccupied with getting back to the mining compound to show any real concern for her.

Echo's conscience berated her again. Ashamed of spying, she dropped lower behind the bushes. Trying hard to regain her shattered self-control, she crept away towards the cabin.

At the center of the stream, Ben rearranged his clothes to speed up the drying process. He smiled to himself as Echo retreated. Thanks to his military training, he had an instinct for knowing when he was under surveillance. He had not spotted her until she moved to leave, but he knew she was watching. The girl's curiosity neither surprised nor bothered him, considering the time she had spent alone in this forsaken place. He doubted he would have done as well.

The bigger problem was his attraction to her. At this stage, he was unsure if it was genuine or just the circumstances, but he had liked her from the moment they met. She was attractive, if a little grimy and a lot naive. Something about the way she handled herself indicated she was very bright and capable. He suspected that once cleaned up, she would also be beautiful.

The girl had guts and an independence of spirit he found appealing, but despite her apparent determination and self-sufficiency, insecurity overshadowed everything else; it was clear she did not want him to leave.

Her obvious interest made his position difficult. He could never be sure if her attention was from genuine curiosity or simply that she needed rescue. The latter was something he could not deal with right now.

Regardless of his personal feelings, she was a civilian survivor and therefore out of bounds. She was his responsibility, but if he failed to get his ship back, they would be stuck on this planet together. On the automatic assumption that the mission had fallen prey to the enemy, another would be a long time in coming.

As he watched Echo disappear into the cabin, a wistful sigh escaped his lips.

Chapter Eight

BEN POINTED TOWARD THE rear of the camp. "See the building over at the back—"

"That's the old assay office." Echo replied.

"Yes, well, the laboratory is in there. Three of those bastards are inside. Two are working on what I think is some kind of bomb, and I'm guessing the other one is creating a biological weapon. There are also lots of other gadgets they are playing around with."

Earlier in the morning, Echo had led the way on the two-hour journey down the animal paths to the valley. With the sun now halfway up the sky, she and Ben lay together on the rocky outcrop above the mining camp.

Motionless, Ben focused his attention on the compound. Echo lay quietly beside him, listening as he spoke. She took comfort from the nearness of him; from having someone else around, someone to talk to and 'be with'.

Last night had not gone at all the way she expected. Ben returned to the cabin before sundown, his clothes washed and his face shaven courtesy of the paring knife.

In the growing dusk, she had dashed down to the stream and taken a quick bath, attempting to wash away her resemblance to a back-alley urchin. Already she was beginning to view this total stranger as a friend, for reasons she could not quite explain. No doubt Ben considered her appearance coarse and uncouth when compared to the women he must have known from other, more sophisticated worlds.

Late into the evening, she had listened to his ramblings. Somehow, she could not focus on the content, so novel was the idea of having someone else around. Now, the following day, she could recall little of what he said. Images remained in her mind, but not the words.

There was mention of the war raging across vast regions of space—a conflict which humanity was losing—and about Ben's plan to rescue his crewmates by arming himself and sneaking back into the mine compound after dark. The detail was lost to her now.

Eventually, he collapsed on the spare mattress and fell asleep, having behaved like a perfect gentleman. That was not what Echo wanted; she had needed company, not a sleeping lump.

Shaking her head, she tried to drag her attention back to the present.

"Biological? How do you know?" she asked, responding to his earlier remarks.

"He works in a sealed-off corner of the lab and always wears an airtight hazard suit. They locked us in a cage just inside the entrance, and I'm guessing they intended us to be the guinea pigs for his experiments. A plague for killing humans, maybe… Whatever they're doing is super dangerous. I'm betting they put the laboratory here in case something got away from them or went wrong. I doubt they think this place would be much of a loss."

"This is—was—my home." Suddenly vulnerable, Echo hunched closer.

Ben could not help but be aware of her closeness. It was clear she had decided he was not an enemy, and the little girl in her now stuck to him like glue, making contact at every opportunity. She was, he realized, starved for companionship. It did not surprise him; in her circumstances, he would have been the same.

"Don't lift too high," he said. "They'll be over here in minutes if they spot us."

"No, they won't. Those monsters don't like coming out here."

Ben grunted an acknowledgement. "The little shed next to the airfield fence… I think that antenna on the roof is what brought us down." He paused for a moment, surveying the compound. "The soldier's barracks and canteen are in those big buildings on the town side, and the small one at the front is the commandant's house and office."

"Yes, I know." Echo groaned, adjusting her position on the rock. "How do you? They locked you in a cage, didn't they?"

"Yeah, but they took us out whenever they needed someone to lift and carry. The Tolleani have a slave society, and they avoid hard work in this sort of heat if they can use prisoners instead."

Echo pointed at a small structure well separated from the others. "The red building over by the edge of the mine apron is the explosives store. My Dad told me about it once. He worked in the…"

"I need to be down there," Ben said, as if oblivious to her words. "I have to get back into my ship."

"The monsters will have figured out how to break in by now, surely. They've probably been right through it."

"I doubt it. I activated the security systems before we stepped onto the tarmac. The second I saw soldiers running from the buildings, I hit the external lock and secured the ship, so the fuselage is live with a massive charge from the reactor. If they touch it, we get alien crisps in a split second. It can't be entered without damaging it, and I don't think they will do that."

"Why not?"

"They want it intact. The commandant tried to force me to deactivate the hull and assigned a guard, just one, to take me back to the airfield. I took the chance to get away and turned on him—put him down before he realized what was happening." Ben edged closer, subconsciously responding to her nearness.

"Funny thing about these guys," he continued. "Despite our technology, they regard us as only moderately intelligent animals, and never consider how we might react. It didn't occur to them I would try to escape; they just assumed I would cooperate."

"Did you kill the guard?"

"Humph."

Echo turned her attention back to the compound. "Good. How did you get away?"

"I ran over the back towards the mine. There's a lake down there…"

"That's where they pump water out of the shafts and store it—stored it—to re-use in the dry season."

"Okay, so there are pipes under the fence where you can squeeze through from the apron. I jumped in the pond and swam across to the far side. The Tolleani won't go in the water, and the fools didn't manage to shoot me. By the time they got around the pond, I was in the trees. I went upstream, crossed back to this side, and headed north, towards the naval station over the mountains."

"And found my cabin instead."

"Yeah, well, I kind of got lost."

Without warning, an ear-splitting roar descended over their heads. Echo shielded her eyes as a colossal spaceship slid by not more than two hundred meters above; a powerful down-blast of hot air almost knocked them from their vantage point.

Back at the tree line, they watched as the vessel settled in front of Ben's ship. At least four times the size of the other Tollean craft, the new arrival's sheer weight drove its landing skids inches into the hard gravel surface, its bulk dominating the landing field. Everything about it marked it as a capital warship.

The boarding ramp dropped, and a handful of aliens disembarked. Two of them crossed to the office, spoke with the guard, and then walked in the direction of the mining compound.

"Shit," Ben cursed under his breath. "My job just got a lot more complex."

"Serves you right for not leaving someone inside your ship, you know," Echo said. "Why did you all get out, for the Gods' sake? That was stupid."

"Yes, you're right, but after months in space, you want to walk about whenever you can, and we thought the place was deserted." Ben did not mention he had disagreed with his captain's decision.

"So, you weren't being careful enough."

"It wouldn't have made much difference. We couldn't have lifted off without resetting the engine circuits. Even if some of the crew had remained inside, none of us would have left without the others."

"Okay, so where do we go from here?" Despite Ben's furrowed brow and grim-set mouth, it pleased Echo that he could not now sneak back to the camp. The need for him to stay with her trumped all else, and whilst she understood his impulse to rescue his ship and crew, the plan was never going to work.

"I'll wait until the cruiser leaves. It might only be a quick turnaround. I'll go down later."

"What if it's here to take your friends away? They won't be there."

For a moment, Ben said nothing, peering down at the alien warship, then, "Yeah, I know."

Echo groaned, rolling on her back. "You're determined to kill yourself, aren't you? You can't get in and out again without being caught, and where is it going to get you? What about me? Once you're dead, I'm stuck here until I die."

A single tear crept down her cheek; gently, Ben reached across to wipe it away. "I'm not going to leave you here, but this is more important than either of us. There's a new weapon down there, and we have to know about it. Do you understand?"

Echo did not reply, fighting to maintain her self-control. "I'm going down to the town," she finally announced. "We need supplies and more food, thanks to you. Come with me. You can't do anything here anyway." Without waiting for a response, she crawled away into the brush. Ben sighed and then followed.

***

Silence hung like a pall over the old settlement as the pair crept through the overgrown gardens at the rear of the buildings.

Echo had not been this close for some time, but she was confident they would not encounter any of the aliens. For a few minutes, she squatted by the hedgerows behind her old home, watching and listening for signs of movement.

Located only a short distance from the PX store Echo intended to visit, the house made a convenient shortcut to the town center. Approaching the corner of the structure, she peered towards the road, making sure they were alone. At the remains of the now overgrown herb garden, she paused by her family's grave markers.

Ben noted the paleness of her face. "Your folks?"

"Yes."

"You buried them yourself?"

"Yes. My mom was inside, and Dad was up at his office. I used a tractor from the mine to bring him here."

"Whose is the third marker?"

"My little brother. He was in the schoolyard." For her, finding Robby and her friends had been the hardest moment of all.

Ben looked down at the graves. He knew well how the Tolleani operated: after murdering every human in a colony, they left as quickly as they came.

Echo wiped a hand across her eyes. Turning away, she struck out towards the PX store with Ben close behind, leaving her family in peace.

"What's that?" Ben pointed to a dull gray patch at the far end of the road.

"I burned the neighbors' bodies. I wanted to dig a grave for them all, but I couldn't drive the big bulldozers from the mine. I gave up on the idea and cremated them instead."

With the return of the monsters, Echo had feared the ash would betray her presence, but the invaders appeared not to care. They stayed in the compound and rarely entered the town.

Ben placed a hand on her shoulder. "At least you gave your people some sort of closure," he said, wiping her cheek with a finger. "Good job." He wondered if it had been the smartest of ideas, but accepted that in her place, he would have done the same.

The supply depot was one of several public buildings and business houses surrounding the small communal plaza, an open dirt space forming the hub of the town.

At the center of the square, a monument stood in memory of the first miners who founded the community. Now the statue was blasted and broken, used for target practice by the aliens during the initial attack. Years ago, Echo researched it out of boredom; one of those men built the cabin she now called home, and dug the exploratory mine in the cliffs behind it.

At the rear of the buildings, she approached a door hidden by a large water tank. "Stay here and keep an eye out," she said, entering without waiting for a response.

Inside the deathly silent building, she took a breath of the fetid air. The conditioners had failed long ago, and a faint, musty odor of decay filled the room. Thick dust, blown in through door cracks and broken window panes, recorded her footsteps as she moved about the floor, picking her way through the dim, cavernous interior.

There were things she needed, more so since Ben was now here. She found shampoo, soap bars, a small mirror, and scissors, placing them in her satchel with the fruit and vegetables gathered on the way into the town. To those, she added safety razors and a shaving stick, expecting Ben might prefer them to a paring knife.

Ignoring the food section—anything remaining there was well beyond being useful—she turned to leave, but stopped when she heard deep, guttural voices from the square outside. Startled, but a little curious, she crept to a front window and peered over the sill.

Nearby, four Tolleani stood in the plaza, turning slowly as they surveyed the buildings. Echo's skin crawled. She detested these creatures to the core of her being, and now they were in her town; she had not seen them here since their return.

One of the intruders was familiar. The distinctive red and green uniform belonged to the camp commandant. Over the last year, he had become the focus of her hatred, for the deaths of her family and friends, and for all the years lost when she should have been making a life for herself.

She did not hold him personally responsible—she had not been close enough to see the alien who shot her father—but this one represented his race, and she had long wished for an opportunity to kill him, or at least try.

A voice in her head screamed she had never had a chance like this before, nor would she again. Chest thumping, she lifted her crossbow towards the window ledge, and then stopped. Her stomach dropped like a lead weight as a hand rested on her shoulder.

"Not the greatest idea," Ben whispered as he knelt beside her. "They're armed, we aren't. You want to get us killed?"

Echo slumped to the floor and struggled to get her nerves back under control. "You frightened the life out of me."

He was right, of course. She could only take out one of them before the others reacted. If she tried, she and Ben would both most likely die. Reluctant to let go so easily, she stole another glance over the ledge.

The monsters stood in a small group near the center of the square, the commandant pointing out various features of the town to his companions, all of whom wore the Tollean version of flight suits. Of all times, Echo thought, the monsters had chosen now for a guided tour.

They appeared human-like, and from the distance of the outcrop, she had at first thought them to be so. Close up, the differences were more obvious. Without doubt humanoid, they had two arms, legs, eyes, and ears, but their hands had four digits with two opposing thumbs, one on either side of two fingers.

Their feet were similar, with one large toe and two smaller ones pointing forward. The second largest digit on each foot, much shorter than the first, pointed out to the side. Both hands and feet had large, black claws. They did not wear shoes, but sandals, form-fitted to their oddly shaped feet.

From the neck up, they were utterly alien. Fine, downy hair covered the skin, their faces devoid of emotion like those of cats. The facial expressions never changed: they neither smiled nor frowned.

The commandant guided his guests across the plaza to one of the funeral pyres, pointed to the blackened patch of ground, and then raised a finger to the forested hillside, prompting a frightening thought to enter Echo's mind.

He knows I'm here. A shiver crawled down her spine as a pair of piercing, yellow, cat-like eyes turned in her direction.

Head down, she crept to the exit. Ben followed, closing the door as they left: an open door would invite investigation, and footprints lay everywhere on the grimy floor.

Halfway to the old homestead, a loud voice barked behind them. A Tollean guard emerged from behind a storage shed and, on seeing them, aimed his rifle and fired. A fountain of dirt erupted beside Echo as the needle blast slammed into the roadway.

With Ben close behind, she dashed down the path at the side of her house. A second shot hit the front wall, sending dry timber splinters in all directions and setting the old, worn structure ablaze. Seconds later, a third impacted the herb garden, ripping into the grave of Echo's family.

Her mind screamed in pain as she vaulted over the remains of the rear fence and into the tall grass. Not until she and Ben disappeared through the hedgerows did the firing cease. By the time the guards reached the fields, no trace of their quarry was visible in the tangle of vegetation beyond.

Chapter Nine

DEEP WITHIN THE FOREST, Echo collapsed and fought to regain her breath. Her confidence shaken and thoughts in turmoil, she realized the commandant now knew of her presence. The ash heaps were faint, washed away by the torrential rains over the years, but the gray stains remained with small pieces of blackened bone scattered everywhere. Echo realized she should have cleaned them up.

Ben dropped to the ground beside her, gasping for breath. "Our friend the commandant is aware of you after all, it would seem."

"How? I stay hidden. The fires?"

"You left plenty of clues: those pyres and your footprints. Whatever else those bastards are, they aren't stupid. He added two and two, is all."

"So why hasn't he come after me before?"

"Lack of interest, I'm guessing. He doesn't view you as a threat, and most likely can't be bothered chasing you without cause. Waste of resources, maybe. The problem is the guard

saw us together, so now they have twice the reason to come after us."

Across the valley, smoke drifted up from the town. Echo's home and the graves of her family, her last real links to this place, no longer existed.

After regaining their breath, she and Ben dragged themselves to their feet and made their way back towards the cabin, thoughts continuing to churn through Echo's mind as they walked. She wondered how she could have been so stupid. The aliens knew of her presence all along and had done nothing. She was little more than a nuisance to them. Not worth the resources. Not important enough to worry about.

***

Later the same afternoon, Echo sat in a shallow pool not far from the cabin. With the overlong rat's nest masquerading as her hair now hacked into reasonable shoulder-length submission, she attempted to scrub away an eternity of accumulated grime. She wished she could wash away her back-planet upbringing so Ben would take more notice, but for now, the dirt would have to do.

Her mother's teachings still lingered in her memory. She remembered how to make herself presentable, and now that she had company, understood for the first time why it was worth bothering. It had never seemed important before.

The life she always anticipated was a distant memory. Despite her always-high expectations as a child, that future was gone, ripped away by a race of monsters she hated with deep-seated conviction.

Until now, it always seemed possible the Tolleani had not known of her presence. Now Echo knew better, that they were prepared to ignore her only as long as she behaved like a good girl and did not upset them, or until they decided to remove her for some obscure reason of their own.

She swallowed hard, attempting to erase the lump in her throat. That she survived only by the forbearance of the aliens infuriated her, but the sudden realization of her unforgivable naivety hurt more.

Forcing her knotted emotions aside, she tried to let go. The late afternoon sun warmed her bare shoulders as she rubbed soap over her skin for the first time in months, letting the stream wash away the pain.

Not far away, Ben walked along the bank deep in contemplation. He glanced up, stopped, waved, and smiled. On returning from the town, he had collapsed on the old mattress, muttering that after weeks in space, full gravity tended to knock a body about. Once he was asleep, Echo thought it safe to clean herself up, but now here he was.

She pretended not to see him until he moved away under the trees. As he vanished towards the cabin, she stole a glance over her shoulder, her face burning from embarrassment. Her discomfort was childish, she realized; he had meant no harm, approaching openly and without hiding, unlike her own earlier adventure. She could hardly criticize, considering.

Scrambling from the water, she stretched out to dry, searching her memory for some sense to today's events. It was strange that this man's intentions should have such a deep effect on her. The hope that he would stay remained strong, but she accepted he had other plans.

All she wanted, had ever wanted, was to remain safe until rescue, but with his vessel lost and little chance of getting it back, Ben could not help her. Even if the aliens knew of her presence, she had been on her own for years and would keep doing so if necessary. She was quite capable of surviving alone and did not need a man to look after her. The other towns would provide a refuge, and in time, another rescue would come.

In the back of her mind, Echo's inner voice whispered otherwise. Ben had been clear about their chances. Getting here at all was fraught with difficulty, and unless he managed to retrieve his spaceship and return home, another vessel might not come this way anytime soon. This might well be her only chance to escape this exile, and so far it was not going well. Perhaps she did need him after all.

The cabin was no longer a haven. If the monsters decided to take the trouble, they would find it with little difficulty. A guard died during Ben's escape, and the soldier in the town spotted him and her together, so they would come eventually.

Ben's presence made her happy. Yesterday, she had laughed for the first time in memory. Right or wrong, every time she thought back to the moment she saw him in the stream, her heart missed a beat.

Rolling on her stomach, she turned her attention to the hut, spotting Ben just outside the door. Once the Tollean ship left, he intended to rush back to the mine unarmed and would be caught and most likely killed. This chance for rescue would be gone, and she would lose the first person to enter her life in years. Echo was not sure which mattered the most to her. At that moment, the path became clearer. To hide alone was no longer an option, and she would not let him leave her behind!

She wished Ben would go with her to a safer place, but that was not going to happen. He would not take her with him to the airstrip, but she intended to accompany him as far as the outcrop. If the aliens caught him—and they would—she would go to his rescue. She did not intend to give him up easily. Assuming the worst-case scenario, she doubted she would dare to kill anyone, even an alien, but if it became necessary, then she would try. If she failed, it was better to die now than starve later.

After sunset, Echo listened as Ben rambled on about his home world. Barely acknowledging the trouble she took to clean herself up, the smile on his face nevertheless betrayed an awareness and appreciation. More than ever focused on his planned mission, he explained his reasons for needing to get back to the ship: his weapons were there, and without the ship, they could not leave under any circumstances. There was no other way off the planet.

"I'll sneak down after dark," Ben said. "I can be in and armed in thirty seconds, and then I can figure out a proper rescue plan for my crew."

"Didn't you say your spaceship was broken?"

"Yeah, but we managed to fix it before they grabbed us. It's almost as if they wanted us to. Everything should be fine now as long as I can destroy whatever shut us down."

"The monsters will be waiting for you." Echo's stubbornness mounted.

"Maybe—maybe not. As far as I can tell, only two guards are stationed at the airfield, and they don't leave the buildings unless they have to. The spaceship crews stay inside. Even though they know I'm here, I doubt they'll post extra sentries. Their mindset is odd."

"That's a little strange, don't you think?"

"Yeah, I suppose, but they think differently from us. Why they react the way they do is beyond me. Despite their advanced technology, they are unbelievably lax, and I figure these local guys are the dregs of their service, sent out here to get them out of some general's hair."

"I still don't get it."

"To them, we're a bit like ants, I think. You see ants running about, and they can bite, invade your home, and so on, but you don't post guards against them, and you don't worry until they become a nuisance. When you spot a solitary ant, you ignore it. We are their ants."

"What are ants?" Echo asked.

After eating, Ben stripped off his flight suit and stretched out on the mattress. With his eyes closed, he attempted to relax and listened to his companion moving about. After a while, he opened his eyes again.

The flames from the stove illuminated the cabin enough to show Echo sitting on the side of the cot. Ben watched her in the flickering half-light. Accepted, she was a civilian and therefore his responsibility, but her effect on him was irrefutable. Despite the sense of duty pecking at the back of his skull, he realized that, depending on his crew, the two of them might be the only humans on this world. In a short time, both of them might be captured or dead.

Echo's dark eyes reflected the dim light from the stove as she turned her head. She seemed small and helpless, with a vulnerability born not from lack of ability but from uncertainty. In a crisis, this young woman behaved as if she were invincible, yet with a complete lack of awareness of her capabilities, she was completely insecure.

"You alright?" he asked.

"Yes, fine … you?"

"Yeah…" In Ben's brain, something slotted into place. Her eyes were focused on his face; she was fascinated by him.

"You can come over here if you want," he said.

Later that evening, Echo burrowed into Ben's arms, talking about how she had survived alone all those years and the moment she first found him in the cabin. Ben listened

attentively, his feelings for this strong and independent, yet self-doubting young woman growing stronger. After she fell asleep, he lay awake for hours, gazing up into the darkness of the roof space, wondering where this would lead.

Chapter Ten

ECHO HAD NO IDEA of the time. Light filtered in through the window and tried to steal past her eyelids as she resisted opening them. For long, dreamy moments she lay motionless, her body pressed hard against Ben's, aware of his steady breathing. With her head on his chest, she listened to his heartbeat. The sound was mesmerizing, something she had not heard since childhood.

"You awake?" Ben whispered.

"Yes. I thought you were still asleep."

"I was until a minute ago. How are you this morning?"

"After last night? Wonderful."

Ben turned his head and gazed at her, an amused expression on his face. "You have no idea what an attractive woman you are, do you?"

"I … never thought… Me?"

"Take my word for it. You're stunning—amazing." He stretched, eased himself to his feet and walked across to the window. "I think we slept kind of late."

Echo screwed her face up. "We shouldn't have done that. I'll probably get pregnant now," she joked.

Ben let out a short, sharp laugh. "That's not going to happen. Spacers are 'fixed' to prevent it."

"How do you mean?"

"Our ships have mixed crews, male and female. The medics give us injections to eliminate any problems."

Echo caught only part of the explanation, focusing on Ben's first few words. "There are women on your ship?"

"My ship? Yes, one, Jill, our communications officer. Best in the service."

Something twisted in Echo's stomach. Women, flying in space, in the Federation fleet! "So, how does a woman get into your space fleet?"

Before Ben could answer, a dull thud hit the cabin. The ancient structure rattled as powerful shock waves shook the old timbers. "Sonic boom," he said, rushing to the door with Echo close behind.

High above the forest canopy, the visiting warship arced across the lower end of the valley towards the ocean, rising into the clouds as it moved away. Within seconds, it disappeared into the upper atmosphere.

"That's my cue," Ben said. "I'm going down to the mine tonight. Time to get my ship back."

Echo's heart sank. "Do you honestly think your crewmates will still be there?"

"No, that warship almost certainly took them, but I have to make sure. Besides, we still need my boat. I can fly it alone if I have to."

For the rest of the morning, she sat on the veranda watching Ben. From a small tree, he cut a long, stout pole and then whittled a sharp tip on the end with his commandeered knife. "Home defense," he explained, thrusting it out in front like a spear. "Gives me a longer reach."

"Really?" Echo tried not to sound too cynical.

At one point, Ben asked to borrow her crossbow, but she refused him. The weapon was the one thing she would not part with. Found years ago in one of the houses of the town, it was her only effective hunting tool; continued survival would be difficult without it.

After the batteries in her laser weapons drained—she never did discover where her father kept the charger at the mine— she had practiced with the bow for days. She could fire a bolt with more accuracy than a pistol blast, and did not intend to lose it when the monsters recaptured Ben and took him away from her.

After noon, he sat down beside her. "I'm leaving now. I'll go down to the airstrip and try to reach my ship. Are you coming with me?"

"No, I'm not," Echo responded without thinking. "You shouldn't go either. I don't want you to go. Not after…"

"I'll be fine. I'm planning on being super careful, trust me. I'll get my weapons and then sneak into the camp. They don't move around a lot in this climate, so I can pick them off one at a time if necessary."

"They'll still catch you. I managed to avoid them for years, and I won't throw that away now. You should stay here."

The second she spoke, she knew it was a mistake. Reluctant as she was to accept it, she understood that as a military officer, Ben had no choice. If he succeeded, they could leave this dreadful place, but if he failed, she would lose him forever and remain trapped on this miserable world. Her biggest fear was not capture but being alone again. "Can we just grab the ship and leave?"

"Yes, we could, but the odds are the Tolleani would bring us down again with that device of theirs; I have to find and destroy that before we can get away. Also, I can't leave if there is any chance my crew is still there."

"I'm sorry. I'll go with you as far as the outcrop. That's all. You're still an idiot."

"Accepted. If all goes well, I'll signal you from the tarmac and you can come down. We could be out of here by morning." Leaning across, he ran his fingers through her hair. "I will come back, but if anything happens, you'll just have to rescue me, won't you?" He leaned in and kissed her lips, and then a grin spread across his face as he rose and headed towards the water.

Echo climbed to her feet and followed, but try as she might, she could not stop the lump from rising in her throat again, or tears from welling in her eyes.

***

Echo and Ben stopped on the ridge above the two enormous Quonset hangars, looking down over the low earth berm that separated the airstrip from the border stream and the surrounding forest.

The office and crew-accommodation blocks by the far gate appeared deserted, but Echo knew better. Nearby, a single, gray Tollean spaceship squatted in the haze, its crew nowhere in sight.

"One of the ships is gone," she said.

"Yeah, it must have left with the cruiser, or we would have heard it. Makes my job easier." Ben lifted up for a better view and pointed towards the fence. "My boat is still there, next to the hydrogen tanks." The black nose of the ship was visible, protruding from behind the nearest hangar.

"Do you think it's still all right?"

"Don't know. Should be, as long as the hull is still sealed. They can't touch it from the outside, and that reactor won't fail for years."

"Can you turn it off?"

"The charge? Yeah, with this," He slapped a hand over the roundel sewn to the breast of his coveralls. "A small transmitter under here lets the ship recognize my presence. All covert-operation flight suits are fitted with them. The power will shut down for twenty seconds if I come within two meters of the external console, long enough to punch in the disable code."

Echo peered down at the airfield. "Lucky they didn't discover it when they caught you."

"Wouldn't have made a difference. Not enough time for them to figure out the sequence. Do you know what's inside those hangars?"

"Nothing much. There's an old spaceship in the big one, but it doesn't work."

Ben's eyebrows arched. "What sort of ship?"

"Don't know—a little one. It's been around as long as I can remember. I used to sneak in and play in it as a kid until my dad found out, then I copped hell. What now?"

"Now we wait for sundown."

"You really think you can get away with this, don't you? There are dozens of those monsters down there. You can't get them all with a stick and a knife. They're going to catch you."

"I don't have to get them. I just need to get on the ship. I'll sneak into the compound later and wreck whatever is in the little building with the antennae. Then I can look for my crew, and maybe try to steal the data storage disk from the laboratory. No one guards the antenna, and there is only one sentry at the lab at night, so all I have to do is take him down and keep my head low. I don't intend to barnstorm the compound. They won't catch me, alright?"

"If they do, I'm coming down after you."

Ben turned towards Echo. A bright pink hue flushed across her face. She was serious; despite all her protests, she would come to his rescue at the risk of her own life. He had not realized his presence meant so much to her.

***

Long fingers of shadow spread across the complex as Ben scrambled down to the stream. Keeping as low as possible, he crawled up the embankment and looked across to his ship, standing isolated and unguarded in front of the hangar. The lack of a guard was illogical, but he had long ago given up trying to understand the inhuman mind of the Tolleani.

As night advanced, a light came on, a single dim lamp illuminating the ground between the administration buildings, the solitary Tollean spacecraft, and the scout cars. The glow extended only partway across the field, sufficient to bathe one side of the Terran craft in half-light, leaving the hangars in virtual darkness.

Derelict machines stood like silent sentries around the edge of the strip. Ben crept through the shadowy monoliths and edged up to the rear of the largest hangar building.

Despite his assurances to Echo, he was not confident of being able to pull this off without being caught or killed. In space, he was a master of his craft, but this was outside his comfort zone. His confidence was a bluff to set the girl's mind at ease, but he suspected that perhaps it had the opposite effect. It would have been wiser to be more honest with her.

Along the outer wall of the hangar, a small side entrance opened to the inside. A faint light broke the blackness inside, leaking out to the cavernous space through a half-closed door in a far back corner.

Ben cursed beneath his breath; one of the Tolleani was working there. That complicated matters. Once his eyes adjusted to the darkness, he made a quick survey of the hangar. It was almost empty, containing only the 'little' ship Echo mentioned and a few ground vehicles.

The craft was a Fleet lifeboat, a standard emergency vehicle designed to carry passengers to safety on the nearest planetary surface. How it got here he could not imagine, but from its appearance, it had been out of service for a long time.

In the almost total darkness, Ben could see little inside the cabin, but these boats were familiar to him. All larger ships carried them, and all followed a similar layout. Unable to see in the faint light filtering through the shuttle's windscreen, he felt around for the control panel. The system was dead, unused for decades.

Satisfied the alien in the back room was still unaware of his presence, Ben grabbed a heavy screwdriver from a nearby workbench and retreated to the door. Once outside, he jammed the tool through the hasp of the exterior lock, hoping it would slow the guard if he chose to follow.

Making the best of the shadow, he sprinted to his ship and crouched by the forward landing strut. Across the airfield, all was quiet; nothing moved by the administration buildings or the alien spacecraft. Hunched low to the ground, trying hard to be inconspicuous, he crept beneath the main hatch.

The exterior control panel sat behind a panel below the entry port, the boarding ladder having withdrawn on activation of the security system. Ben moved closer, taking care not to touch the hull, until a red light on the panel flickered to green and the panel opened silently.

Seconds later, satisfied his beautiful vessel remained untouched and ready to fly, he hit the disable button and waited for the boarding ladder to descend. The ship appeared safe, the only visible damage a slight buckling of the hastily extended skids sustained during the slide across the tarmac. So far, all was going to plan.

***

Echo maintained her vigil, sitting in darkness on the hillside. Legs drawn up to her chin, she wrapped her arms around her knees and waited. Her stomach churned with a dread feeling. Something was wrong.

Instinct told her this expedition must end in tragedy, but Ben had ignored her misgivings. As intelligent as he might be, it occurred to her he did not think things through as well as she expected of a fleet officer. Perhaps 'duty' trumped common sense.

He gave the impression of total competence in everything he did, and presumably it was true in his own environment. Here on the ground, the wisdom of some of his decisions seemed doubtful. Battling to ignore her fears, she again tried to put a precise finger on why his actions troubled her so, and subconsciously held her breath.

Unbidden, the confrontation in the town rushed back into her mind. If the monsters came looking for her, she could still move to one of the other settlements. The Tolleani never went there, and if they did, she could always hide in the caves that riddled the mountains along this coastline. If Ben failed—

A deep sense of despair returned as she realized her plans were an illusion.

Ben's arrival had changed everything. This man was the lifeline to which she had chosen to attach herself. He represented the one chance of escape from this exile. Moreover, she had promised she would go after him if necessary.

A faint movement drew her attention. Down on the poorly lit airfield, she could barely make out Ben's small figure crouched in the shadows by the nose landing gear of the black ship.

More movement appeared on the far side of the airstrip. From behind the administration block, three monsters stepped into the pool of light beneath a window, stood in a cluster and talked among themselves.

At first, she wondered what they were saying, then realized that while she could see them from her higher vantage point, Ben could not. She prayed they would stay near the barracks.

The Tolleani did not move. Ben stepped out of sight, reappearing soon after by the nose wheel. At the back of the hangar, a door opened, visible only by the dim light leaking out onto the ground. A bulky shape appeared and moved around the outside of the building. A sudden chill ran down Echo's spine.

A monster had been inside all along and was now sneaking out by a rear door. Ben was unaware he was being stalked from behind. Echo hoped the alien was acting alone and had not raised the alarm in some way.

A moan escaped her lips as she realized her prediction would come true unless she did something to prevent it. She could not abandon Ben. It was more than getting off this planet; she liked this beautiful man who had walked unannounced into her life. If she did not want to lose him, she would have to act, despite her better judgment. Bow in hand, she slipped over the rocks towards the stream-bed.

Chapter Eleven

FROM BEHIND THE LANDING skid, Ben looked across to the administration block. Something moved, but he could not be sure. So far, no sound had come from the workshop, the worker in the back presumably still unaware of his intrusion.

A deep, guttural voice shattered the silence. Ben spun to see a Tolleani run from the corner of the hangar. The alien, barely visible in the night, lumbered towards the spacecraft.

Slamming his hand onto the security activation switch to secure the ship, Ben then moved to put the skid between him and the new arrival. With an object that looked like a plasma-pulse rifle in hand, the guard posed a serious threat. A blinding blue-green ball of flame lashed out, slamming into the port under-wing landing strut.

Time paused. A creaking sound came from the wing, followed by a long, drawn-out rending as the gear, glowing hot from the blast, began to fail. Without hesitation, Ben launched himself beneath the hull and out under the opposite side.

As an engineer, he understood exactly what effect the plasma burst had on the ship and what would follow. The strut, normally protected within the shell of the vessel whilst in space, was not armored in itself. Within seconds, the metal reached the limits of its heat-weakened state and buckled. The hull lurched to one side, the port wing splitting as it thudded down with a sickening crunch.

Picking himself up from the ground, Ben stared at the wreck of his beloved spacecraft. The far side of the fuselage was not visible from where he stood, but it did not need to be. The scream of tortured titanium said everything. Its skin breached, the spacecraft would not fly again without major repairs. The only ticket off this accursed planet was gone.

Another growl reached him from the rear of the stricken vessel. The alien, having rushed forward during the collapse, stood near the stern, weapon raised and aimed.

A faint bell sounded: the crash had triggered an alarm. Across the tarmac, three Tolleani ran around the end of the administration building as a door opened at the front and two more figures emerged.

Not good, Ben thought. Capture had always been a possibility, but not so easily or quickly. He had been stupid; the girl had figured it right.

Unsure where to go, he turned his attention back to his attacker. The alien stood with feet apart, arms outstretched, only meters away. He held not the plasma rifle but a smaller laser pistol, the rifle now on the ground beside him. Just as well, Ben thought. There was no way a human body could survive a plasma bolt hit.

It seemed impossible to Ben that he could evade the laser shot either.

He lurched to one side as the guard fired, a sharp pain ripping through his leg where the beam grazed his flesh. From a distance at which he would never have missed a target, his attacker had done exactly that.

The Tollean stood motionless, then stiffened. The weapon slipped from his hand as his arms dropped to his side. Body buckling, he slumped to his knees and fell forward, face down. In the dim light, a short, thin shaft protruded from his back.

"Run," a familiar voice yelled. Echo sprinted from behind the wreck, crossbow in hand. She ran to her victim and kicked away his pistol, then sprinted towards her man. "They're coming, behind you," she screamed as she grasped Ben's hand and fought to drag him away.

A hundred meters distant, five soldiers loped across the field. Alerted by the alarm, they saw their comrade fall and the two humans bolt into the shadows before disappearing into the darkness by the hangar.

One arm under Ben's, Echo supported him as they ran past the Quonset, through the machinery graveyard at the rear, and into the stream bed. The dense underbrush on the far bank swallowed them as they vanished headlong into the surrounding trees.

Not until a significant stretch of forest lay between themselves and the airfield did they stop to check if the aliens had followed. Minutes later, both collapsed on the outcrop from where they had earlier reconnoitered the compound.

"How can you be so stupid?" Echo spat.

"Yes, you're right." Ben gasped, sucking air into his tortured lungs. "I wasn't as prepared as I thought. Why didn't you grab his pistol?"

For a moment, Echo's face looked blank. "Didn't think to," she replied.

In the distance, the airfield lights now blazed, the strip alive with soldiers. One group stood at the edge of the water, looking across to the place where their quarry had vanished. Behind them, two more figures walked around the hangar. The guards snapped to attention as they approached.

"Our beloved commandant," Ben said.

"They didn't come after us."

"No. I guess you were right there too. They don't like to go into the forest; they won't do that at night."

"They're not going to chase us?"

"I'm sure they will, but not now. Maybe they won't leave the compound after dark under any circumstances, but in the morning... We should hide."

Back beneath the tree canopy, Echo attempted to examine Ben's leg in the darkness, feeling a slick wetness. The left side of his flight suit felt charred, with blood soaked through the cloth below the knee. "You're hurt."

"Yeah—not too bad, I think. That's not the worst, though."

"What?"

"The bastard you shot wrecked my ship. It was our only way off this planet."

***

Barbus Koll stood on the earth bank separating the edge of the airstrip from the perimeter stream, and glared at the forest opposite. He did not intend to send his men into that hellhole at night, but tomorrow would be a different matter.

Until now, the escaped human had not concerned him. It was one less animal to worry about, and he had doubted its ability to survive for long. The situation had now changed.

Two humans ran from the airfield, indicating the prisoner and the creature from the hillside were together and confirming the report from the soldier in the town. The guards also claimed the one with long hair, the smaller one, killed his best mechanic. This time, the little animal had taken a step too far.

Koll jumped down from the bank, determined to track the human down and destroy both her and her new friend. Directing his men to recover the corpse of the rating, he walked back towards the compound.

Command would insist on an accounting, a detailed description of this disaster, including any consequent actions taken. Koll had already reported the escapee dead, so this could not be blamed on him. It would be better to accuse the fool mechanic of destroying the ship and killing himself while testing a poorly repaired plasma weapon. The guards had found the discarded rifle lying on the ground near the body; indications were that it had burned out after a single shot. He could blame the whole incident on shoddy workmanship.

With no other official vessels due for weeks, the corpse could be disposed of in the base furnace. Blame the mechanic, destroy the evidence, and deal with the problem of the humans separately and quietly.

As he passed, he glanced across to the wreck. It was as well the idiot guard was dead. It served him right for damaging such a beautiful machine. A small fire now flickered beneath the damaged wing, and Koll knew it was only a matter of minutes before the wreck exploded. Time to get clear as quickly as possible. Shouting orders to shut down the nearby refueling pumps, he stalked towards the gate to the compound.

Until the coordinator of the command ship had informed him otherwise, Koll had intended to keep the vessel for himself as a spoil of war. Such a beautiful thing, if only he could've gotten inside.

Back at his office, he cursed Command for lumbering him with the most incompetent, inept guards imaginable.

***

The journey back to the canyon took twice as long as normal; Ben needed constant support while scrambling along the stream bank. The laser slash on his calf bled a little, but the muscle and bone had escaped serious damage, with the wound mostly sealed by the heat of the beam.

Echo wrapped it with a strip of cotton cloth torn from the bottom of her shirt. When they reached the cabin, both collapsed on the mattress.

"Now maybe you will listen to me," Echo said.

"I'm sorry, okay? I won't make that mistake again."

Echo lay back and stared up at the roof. "Alright, my shining knight. What's your next foolproof plan?"

Ben ignored the sarcasm. "We can't stay here. The bastards will come for us first thing in the morning."

"This hut is hidden under the trees. They won't find us that easily."

"Yes, they will. Those scout cars use heat seekers. The only reason they didn't come after you before is that you weren't a problem for them. You shot a guard. With the one I killed while escaping, that makes two; the commandant is not going to take that sitting down."

"Oh, Gods." Echo held a hand to her mouth. "I did, didn't I! I never killed anyone before. But I had to, or you'd be a prisoner now."

"No, I would be dead now, and I'm forever grateful to you for preventing that. That guard only missed because you shot him the instant he hit the trigger."

Ben leaned over and kissed her on her cheek. Without doubt, what had occurred distressed her, but he was sure she would cope. She was a strong woman despite her misgivings.

"Think of it as killing an animal, a monster, as you call them. Just like hunting, yes?"

"Yes, of course, but…" Echo breathed in and then let out a deep breath. "I guess so." She lay back on the mattress, her mind in confusion. Angry with Ben for his carelessness, she was also furious at herself for being so stupid as to get into this predicament.

It was impossible to go down to the town again; the Tolleani would be watching. Yes, they would find this cabin with little difficulty, so she and Ben needed to hide.

Despite the consequences, her actions had not been optional. This man was too important to her now, and they were in this together, whatever the outcome.

"They regard us as animals," he said. "Consider them the same way. They show no compunction whatever about killing us."

"They caught you quickly enough. I thought you were supposed to be a warrior."

"Granted, but I'm a spacer and engineer, not a soldier. This is not my element. I fly ships. I don't fight in ground combat. That little effort was stupid, I admit, and I'm sorry." Ben lifted a hand and stroked Echo's hair. "The good thing for us is they don't like ground battles much either. They attack only when conditions suit them, and with superior force. If things aren't right, the bastards wait until they are, so we won't see them until daylight."

For a few minutes, they lay in silence, and then Ben sat up and wrapped his arms around his knees, withdrawn into his thoughts.

"We have to leave here," Echo said.

"And go where? I relied on being able to steal my boat back. That's not possible now. The shell split when the wing hit the ground. That explosion we heard just after we got away was almost certainly her. She's gone, and I still need to find my crew."

"The spaceship took them. Face it."

"Most likely, yes, but I have to be sure. I can't abandon them without at least checking."

"Can the monsters' heat thingy read through solid rock?"

"No, the sensors have limitations."

"Then we can hide in the tunnels."

"What?"

"The ridge behind us contains an extensive cave system, and a mine shaft behind this hut leads into it. It's an old exploratory dig, the reason they built this cabin here in the first place. The miners abandoned the workings when they broke through into the cave network. I set up an emergency refuge in there, in case."

"When the Tolleani discover us, they'll find the tunnel, won't they?"

"Not likely. The entrance disappeared under a cliff collapse decades ago. My dad used to prospect here on his days off, and he dug a secondary passage back inside. It's well hidden; you can only find your way in if you know where to look."

"Perfect. We need to go now. Heat seekers won't be able to locate us under solid rock."

"In the morning. You said they won't start before then, and it will take them time to find this place. You need to rest."

"Yes, but…" Now that Ben had stopped running, his body refused to obey further. Exhausted from the pain of his wound and by the gravity, he was in no condition to argue. "Alright, first light then. We'll hear them coming, so we should be safe enough. Can't hide in the caves forever, but they'll do for now."

"Then we can go to one of the other towns. The monsters don't go there."

For a moment, Ben sat staring at the ceiling. "The settlement on the other side of these mountains… I saw a military airbase there. We flew over it before those bastards brought our ship down."

"Yes, I've been there."

"Several space planes are sitting on the tarmac, but all are damaged."

"I know. After the attack, I went looking for help. There's nobody left—all dead. I searched the whole place."

"How long will it take to go there on foot?"

"By road? About two days of hard walking. Four, with your leg."

"No, we can't follow the road. They'll be looking for us. Can we go over the mountains?"

"No. These hills are all ridges and gorges, impossible in your condition."

Ben did not reply, instead lowering his head deep in thought. Later, as he slept, Echo remained wide-awake, too wound up to rest. For the last few hours, she had felt strangely exhilarated, and it troubled her. Despite revulsion at all she had done, the realization dawned that she had enjoyed the excitement. After years of boredom, life was exploding around her, and as loath as she was to admit it, it excited her.

Leaning across Ben's body, she checked to see if he was still awake—a loud snore sent her rolling back to the other side of the mattress.

The next morning, they woke to the sun streaming through the trees outside the cabin window. A loud whine filled the air.

"Shit!" Ben said, stumbling to his feet. "A scout. They'll find us soon, if they haven't already. We need to get out now."

Chapter Twelve

ABOVE THE FOREST CANOPY, one of the small scout cars from the airfield hovered, the crew's eyes glued to the screen of a thermal scanner. Below, a mountain stream cut a swath through the unbroken vegetation at the bottom of a ravine they had followed from the lower valley floor. It was the third gorge they had explored since dawn.

On either side of the waterway, pinpoints of heat moved beneath the trees, marking the locations of small native creatures as they scurried away from the noise and the downdraft. Nearer the canyon wall, two larger signatures appeared side-by-side.

Under-Leader Brask barked orders at his pilot, confident he had found his target. Good guess, he thought. Any animal needed water to survive, so they had to be hiding along one of the watercourses.

Ben looked up through the trees from the veranda as the aircraft hovered above. "Come on. It's moving back to make an attack. That bastard's going to fire on us."

"No, through here—hurry," Echo yelled. At the rear of the cabin, she grabbed what was at hand and stuffed it into her satchel. Shoving the mattress aside, she exposed a large, square trapdoor.

Ben cursed beneath his breath as he dashed back inside, slamming the door behind him.

The target confirmed, the scout hovered motionless, its nose facing the direction of the sensor contacts. Missiles streaked from its side pods, sending a rolling, orange and black ball of fire across the cliff face as they impacted the cabin. No sooner had they hit than two more followed, and again, until the forest in all directions vanished in a hellish conflagration of licking flames and roiling black smoke.

For twenty minutes, the crew of the alien craft waited as the fire raged over the floor of the gorge. The sensors were useless now, showing nothing but blanketing heat, but instinct told Brask the projectiles had hit their mark.

Nothing could survive the firestorm. The targets were in the impact zone when the missiles launched, and could not have escaped. Satisfied he could report success to the coordinator or at least avoid his wrath, Brask flung another order at the pilot. The small ship turned and roared down the valley towards the sea.

From a small, almost invisible opening high on the gorge wall, Echo looked out over the inferno, struggling to catch her breath in the smoky air and thanking the Gods her father had closed the mine entrance years ago to keep other explorers away.

Wishing to retain access to the caves, he had dug a deep trench from the cabin to the cliff face and then tunneled through it into the old mine shaft, covered everything visible with timber and earth, and allowed the vegetation to grow back. The only way from the canyon floor into the diggings and the caves beyond was through the entrance beneath the mattress.

When Echo realized the scout's intentions, she grabbed her crossbow and bag and made a dive for safety. By the time the missiles slammed into the hut, both she and Ben were safe, protected by a meter of logs and soil. A shock wave hammered through the tunnel as the trap door imploded and knocked them flat, but thanks to the cabin collapsing under the force, the heat and flames did not reach them.

Once inside the mine, Echo lit an oil lamp and picked her way through to the cave network, then scrambled up to her present vantage point. From there, hidden from all but direct view, she watched the Tollean ship quarter the area then move away, leaving blackened devastation in its wake.

Lying prone on the rock lip, she looked down into the gorge. Her heartbeat increased, breaths coming in short gasps. She wondered if the fire was affecting her. Adrenaline coursed through her body just as it had the previous night at the airstrip.

Oh, Gods! The excitement … near-death excites me, she thought. No, that's ridiculous. Sucking in another breath, she tried to calm herself. The idea that the encounter aroused her was too much at that moment.

Her companion squeezed in beside her. "What now? You look a bit flushed."

"Follow me", Echo responded, ignoring his observation. Crawling from the opening back along the narrow cave passage towards the mine, she struggled to compose herself and act as calmly as possible.

At one point, the old diggings broadened into a wider area with a level floor, the walls and roof lined with old timbers. Another mattress lay against a wall, surrounded by cooking equipment, oil lamps, and crates of assorted gear.

"This is where the original prospectors lived before they built the hut," she said, placing her lamp on an old barrel. "My dad and I cleaned the place up years ago, and I restocked for emergencies when I moved here last year."

Clever girl, Ben thought. "You anticipated this?"

"I expected the monsters to come looking if they ever discovered me. I was wrong. They never did."

"Yeah, until now." Ben sat on the mattress. "If you hadn't done this, we would have been trapped in that fireball. Now all we need is to get out of here and figure out a way off this planet."

Echo put aside her bag and crossbow and dropped beside him. "What about the monsters' ships?"

"No, the big one is out. I've never flown one of those, and I can't read the controls or manuals. The scout cars I might figure out, but they're atmospheric—can't travel in space."

Echo lay back, thoughts rushing through her mind in a constant, confused flood. "We can't leave until the fires burn out."

"How come there is no smoke in here?"

"The wind in the canyon sucks air through these tunnels and out; the smoke goes with it."

Ben nodded, closing his eyes. Echo stared at the walls of the mine, angry at the loss of the cabin and still edgy from her recent experiences. The caves were hotter than normal, but she was not convinced that was the cause of her perspiration.

"I didn't sleep last night," she said. "You snored right through."

"Sorry. Like I said, this gravity knocks me about a lot."

For what seemed like an eternity, they lay in silence until Echo rose and began to rummage through the supplies in the crates. She understood the ship's loss upset Ben: it was not only their way off the planet, but also his pride and joy. He had been second in command and the chief engineer, and had lost his much-loved baby. A thought leaped into her mind.

"You're an engineer, yes?"

"Yeah, right."

"So you can repair a ship?"

"Yes, of course, but not a wrecked one lying on an alien-occupied airstrip."

"What about the ships at the base along the coast?"

"Like I said, the Tolleani blasted them from the air when they first arrived. I don't think they'll ever fly again."

"The one in the hangar?"

"I'm sorry?"

"The spaceship inside the building at the back of the field —the hangar in the back corner."

Ben sat up and leaned forward, his eyes fixed on Echo's. He tried to think back to his flyover and whether or not the roof of that particular structure had been damaged. "This ship is space-worthy?"

"I don't know … don't think so. The controls inside are all pulled apart. It looks like they were fixing something. Maybe you could finish it."

"Perhaps, if it isn't too much of a mess."

"Then we can leave."

"Yeah, but I will still have to come back here first."

"Why?" Echo shook her head with frustration. "Can't we just go? Your crew are gone, damn it."

"Very likely, but I have to make sure. And I'm going to find out what the bastards are doing in that base."

Echo's vision began to blur again. "Why is that so damned important?"

"I'm sorry, but we need to know what they are developing. It might be critical for the war effort."

"Why?"

"Ask yourself. Why would they put a project way out here at the end of nowhere? The work would be so much easier on one of their home planets, but instead, they come here to a remote world they left for dead. It has something to do with the stuff in the mine, I'm sure, and the research is so dangerous they don't dare do it on one of their worlds."

"Trilatenite … the 'stuff' is Trilatenite. Can it be turned into a weapon?"

"Not one I've ever heard of, but I'm an engineer, not a physicist. Fusion reactors use it, so I wouldn't be surprised. There's a data block in their lab; every night, they remove it from their computer and lock it away in a safe. I want it."

Echo sniffed and returned to her rummaging. Arguing did not seem worthwhile. "Okay, we go to the airbase, fix the spaceship, and come back here. This time I help. I know their movements better than you do. We rescue your friends if they are still there and steal your computer block." With any luck, she thought, by the time the ship was fixed, he would change his mind about coming back here at all.

Ben sat watching as she moved about the grotto. "So, how long did you think for us to get there overland?"

"In this area, high ridges run down to the sea with lowlands between them. There are several between here and the air base. We could never cross them with your leg the way it is. In your condition, our only choice is to follow the road."

"So you said before. How long?"

"It'll take us several days on foot, and it's more exposed. The valleys are all low grassland and marsh, and there isn't much cover. Where the mountains come down to the coast, they're covered with forest, and that's better for concealment.

At one place, there's a cave we can shelter in, and we can do the open areas at night."

"The Tolleani use heat sensors," Ben said, "so they will see us either way, except in the cave. The good news is, at the moment they think we're dead, so they won't be looking."

"Fine," Echo said, dumping an old metal plate of suspect-looking cold food on the floor in front of Ben and sitting beside him. "It's only a sort of dried biscuit. I'll get some other supplies together, then we leave."

Ben liked this young woman. He picked up the dish, examined the contents, and tried to decide exactly what it was.

***

Through the night, the fire burned higher towards the peaks, petering out as it tried but failed to compete with the saturating dampness of the forest. In its wake, it left the stream hemmed by a carpet of ash and charred tree trunks, the ruins of the cabin a blackened pile of burned timbers.

The next morning, the ground still smoldered in many places, but the water ran clear, washed clean overnight. Most of the smoke was gone. With the entrance tunnel collapsed by the explosions, what little had reached the caves drifted away from the refuge with the natural ventilation of the honeycombed ridge.

Towards midday, Echo helped Ben down from the opening high in the cliff face to the floor of the canyon and then followed the gorge towards the coast, emerging below the town.

She knew the way to the next settlement well, having driven the coastal route several times after the Tollean attack, in search of other survivors. As darkness settled over the coastline, she and Ben set off for the air base, their way lit by the pale light of Corros's twin moons.

The road wound its way along the coastline just behind the dunes. Unused for years, it was now little more than a track, covered in water-worn potholes, vegetation encroaching at the edges. In many places, sand drifts or water covered the surface, but going on foot was better than Echo had expected. Traveling through the night, they crossed the first ridge and descended to the next valley.

The following day, they sheltered in a copse of woods not far from the path, spending the daylight hours huddled beneath an old foil thermal blanket from the mine. It provided respite from the sun and at least some protection against detection by alien heat sensors.

Echo enjoyed the time being close to another person, not only for the intimacy but also from a need for simple companionship. She missed the embraces of her parents and brother, and each hour brought her closer to Ben.

Increasingly, the idea intensified that she was reliant on him, not only to escape the planet but also for strength, reassurance, and peace of mind. That he was not at his best on the ground was something she could forgive; he was, no doubt, superb in his own environment.

The next afternoon, they stopped in deep forest where a second ridge ran down to the ocean. At a creek crossing, Echo guided Ben upstream to where water flowed from a cave opening in the cliffs. Beyond a mound of boulders, the entrance led away into darkness.

"There's a ledge in there where we can camp beside the stream," Echo said. "The heat seekers won't be able to find us, and we're too far away for them to see smoke, so we can build a fire."

She picked her way over the rocks to a narrow shelf deeper inside the ridge. Through the evening, they lay close together on the rock floor, not for warmth, but for a sense of comfort and safety.

"This is a good spot," Ben murmured. The last twelve hours had been difficult for him. He was a big, heavy man, and Echo had supported him all day, his leg troubling him more with each passing hour. The wound, despite being only shallow, had begun to fester. Infection was rare on this world, and it was something Echo felt powerless to deal with.

As she lay back, she gave in to exhaustion. No more ... not today.

***

Soon after dawn on the fifth day, they reached the next settlement. Typical of the mining colonies on this planet, it was an open plaza surrounded by a handful of public and community buildings, with the residential quarters along secondary roads leading out from the town center. Like Echo's home, this one served a single mine located further away in the surrounding hills.

Human remains lay everywhere in the streets. With no survivors to collect, bury, or burn them, the victims of the Tollean attack remained where they fell, disturbed over the years by roaming animals.

On the approaches, Echo counted numerous skeletons in the stock pens. In her valley, she had released the domestic animals, but here, any that failed to break free on their own remained trapped until overtaken by death. She had visited this place a month after the Tollean attack and had released a few still living animals, but at that stage, most had already died.

During the long and arduous journey, Ben's injured leg had worsened each day. Upon reaching their objective, they searched for anything that might help. Beneath its bandages, the wound was inflamed, the muscles red, swollen, and painful. In Echo's experience, the local microbes were ineffective on the bolstered human immune system, but the normal rules did not seem to apply now.

"Immunity here is based on technology, and it's a fragile thing," Ben said. "Take away the foundation, and the structure tumbles. This infection might be anything, a mutation maybe, or something Tollean."

He had not received the treatments given to the colonists, so it could even be something local. Whatever it was, broad-spectrum drugs might work, or not. Most colonies' PXs stocked a small supply of them, but it would depend on whether they were still viable."

With no obvious signs on the buildings surrounding the square to guide them, Echo began a door-to-door search. The PX contained nothing useful, but in what proved to be the town doctor's office, she found a variety of medications, long past their use-by dates but with luck still effective. She doubted the antibiotics would work, but Ben's response to the anti-inflammatory drugs and analgesics was positive, so they rested for a few days until the redness in the leg subsided.

Their destination, the deserted naval air base, was now only a few kilometers distant.

Chapter Thirteen

SOON AFTER DAWN ON the eighth day, Echo and Ben stopped on a rise overlooking the military base. The ruined facility looked deserted in the bright morning light, shrouded by a deathly silence.

Inside the perimeter fence, the damaged patrol ships sat side by side in front of the hangars. Except for one, which had burned, the hangar buildings appeared untouched at first, their doors closed. From the high ground, signs of alien attack were visible on the roofs of almost all the others.

Ben began the climb down towards the road. "Doesn't look like anyone's around. It's as quiet as a tomb down there."

The front entrance was wide open; only an old and worm-eaten wooden boom blocked the way. The gatehouse was a blackened ruin. Inside the yard few of the smaller structures remained standing, the offices and living quarters reduced to piles of charred timber.

Without bothering to check the buildings, Ben limped out to the tarmac to inspect the patrol vessels. "I guess we can forget about them. Control decks are gone, and one engine is blown out on the second. What wasn't destroyed by laser fire has been ruined by the rain getting in. Neither will ever fly again."

"The monsters just left them here," Echo said. "They don't waste much time on things, do they?"

"No, but it makes sense. The ships are wrecks, so the bastards have no interest in them. They can't use them, and any of our technology they might have been interested in would have been crisped when they blew out the cockpits, so why bother? Stupid really, to hit the cockpits like that. Show me where this other boat is."

Echo led him across the airfield to a slightly smaller hangar located in the furthest corner of the compound. A personnel door opened into one side of the building, and a massive lock hung from the latch bolt.

"It was padlocked when I came here before," she said, "but I smashed it to get in. This one is new. The monsters must have been here."

Minutes later, Ben returned from one of the other hangers with a heavy steel wrench, and within seconds, the new lock lay in pieces. He wondered why the Tolleani had put it there. Perhaps they were interested in the ship Echo claimed was within.

The interior of the hangar lay in semi-darkness, but as Ben's eyes adjusted to the low light filtering in through long-uncleaned skylights, a solitary object emerged from the gloom. "Well, I'll be... Christ on a bicycle!"

"What?"

"This is a military courier. Super fast, three-man flyer designed for carrying dispatches and emergency supplies. Similar to my ship but smaller, and a lot older. What in the Gods' names is it doing here?"

"Can we use it to get away?"

"For sure, if it's space-worthy."

The vessel was about thirty meters long, sleek and metallic gray, the long, tubular fuselage sporting short, stubby wings for atmospheric flight. With no windows anywhere, it resembled a sinister and deadly missile.

A work platform stood under one of the wing cowlings, access panels folded back to reveal the mechanisms within. Ben climbed up and peered inside for several minutes. "They must have been swapping in a new engine—got it in but not hooked up. I can see better when I get some light in here." He scrambled down again, ambled over to the boarding ramp, and climbed inside the fuselage.

Echo moved to follow and then stopped: she knew nothing about these ships or anything mechanical. Everything in there would be beyond her understanding, so she turned and left the hangar, intent on exploring the compound.

Most of the unburnt buildings showed major roof damage; only the maintenance workshop and a handful of smaller structures had escaped destruction. As Echo started to cross the courtyard, Ben walked up beside her, pointing towards a small, still intact building by the gate. "The base commander's residence."

"Why are some buildings damaged and not others?"

"The Tolleani employ a standard technique when they attack a military ground target. They use heat sensors to locate personnel from the air, and take each one out with a needle beam. That usually sets fire to the building, but some escape being fired on because they are vacant at the time. It might be what saved our courier. The bastards may be murdering arseholes, but they aren't needlessly destructive—usually."

"These were," Echo said, looking at the surrounding ruins. "Is the spaceship all right?"

"No, but it can be, given time. The engine installation will have to be completed, the control console needs rewiring, and the fuel tanks are empty. The main batteries are flat, so the computers are down, and most of the systems will have to be checked over as well. It looks like it was just being given a routine overhaul when the attack occurred."

"Can you fix it?"

"Yes. It won't be easy on my own, but I can do it. All our ships have multiple backup systems, so the computers are restorable. The refueling station still has a sealed underground storage with liquid hydrogen inside … a win for us."

"I can help. I don't know machines, but I can still lift and carry. And I can find us food while you work."

"Perfect," Ben replied. "What would I do without you?

***

Weeks later, Echo sat on the porch of the residence. They had assumed the building escaped destruction because it was empty at the time of the alien attack, but on closer inspection, they found foil insulation lining the roof. The metal interfered with heat-sensing equipment like a thermal blanket; the structure would have appeared vacant regardless.

She soon discovered her earlier belief that the monsters rarely came here was wrong. Once a week, a scout car flew over the town and base, and on each occasion circled before heading inland toward the third of the mining communities: it was clear the aliens kept at least a cursory eye on the settlements.

Avoiding the flyovers was easy. As soon as the whine of engines reached her ears, Echo ducked for cover, having already found all the places she would be safe from detection. Ben spent most of his time in the maintenance hangar and always sheltered in the fuselage of the dispatcher.

The scouts were easy to detect when they came during the day, but at night, when one slept, the risk was always greater. At first, Ben suggested they stay inside the ship, then decided the commander's residence, with its insulated walls and ceiling, would provide a safer and more comfortable haven. It was now their refuge and temporary home.

It seemed an eternity since they had arrived at the base. Ben insisted the repairs, whilst a much bigger job than first expected, were 'do-able', and whenever he needed a third and fourth hand, Echo helped as best she could. Most of the time, his head remained buried in a console somewhere, and at those times, she busied herself with the task of keeping them both alive and fed, leaving him to concentrate on his work.

She spent most of her time on the porch of the residence, watching the entrance to the base and the road to the town. If the aliens came to check on the place physically, they would come by air or by that road. Given enough time, she could warn Ben.

Often she hung around the hangar even when not needed, to provide moral support and just be close. Sometimes she wished he could spend more time with her; the memory of him standing in the stream entered her mind more and more frequently with each passing day. Daydreams would drift through her mind, and then she would remember he was up to his armpits in manuals and wiring.

Once in a while, she walked down to the settlement. A reasonable supply of still edible foodstuffs remained in the PX, a carton of packed rice and various other dried items, and the odd can that still looked safe. Technology had not yet failed them completely. As in her town, the farms here had grown wild but still contained edible vegetables and fruit.

Meat was a different matter. Unlike her home, this settlement did not have a river close by, and over the years, most animals managing to free themselves had migrated to distant water sources like the dam at the head of the town's supply pipeline, miles away in the foothills of the great coastal ranges. The need to drag a carcass so far home made hunting there impractical.

Only one water source existed nearby. On the hillside behind the hangars, a large, concrete tank, gravity fed by the pipeline from the dam, serviced the airbase. The system was still functional, and once Echo got the taps in the residence unfrozen, she had good, clean water.

With no electricity—the only usable generator was in the workshop, commandeered by Ben for his work—she used a portable gas cooker to heat water. After so many years of washing in a cold stream, it felt good to take a warm bath, something even Ben appreciated.

Some usable weapons also surfaced. In a military establishment, it was inevitable guns would be found somewhere, and everywhere she went, she kept a sharp eye out.

During the original attack, fire from ships hundreds of meters overhead had cut down the base personnel before they could identify their attackers, and many weapons now lay corroded and useless in the open, scattered with the bones of their owners. Echo collected them for Ben's examination, but it was a wasted effort.

Inside the remaining buildings, she found three laser rifles and a collection of needle guns, all with flat power cells but still serviceable. With a jury-rigged trickle device from the generator to recharge the batteries, several were now functional.

Her best discovery came from an underground ordinance bunker hidden behind high concrete walls at the far corner of the airfield. As with the hangar, an alien lock secured the massive main door, but the device was no match for a sledgehammer from the workshops.

Inside stood rack upon rack of weaponry, the ordinance of the base ranging from missiles to small hand-held grenades. How the stockpile escaped destruction, Ben could not fathom, but again, the fact that the Tolleani had inspected and secured the store concerned him, proof as it was that the aliens did come to this place at least occasionally. After a thorough search, he retrieved a carton of explosive mines, which now sat in one of the rooms of the residence.

"These are called 'daisy-chains,'" he said, juggling one of the small donut-shaped objects in his hand. "They're designed for tactical ground work. A couple of them can reduce a ship to scrap metal."

Ben pointed to the front of the device. "If you turn the dial clockwise,"—he indicated a series of five numbers around the right-hand side—"you set it to a specific frequency for the radio trigger—this thing here—and you can work five different sets of charges off the same control by using different frequencies. Anti-clockwise, and you have an auto timer for anything up to ten hours. Connect them with these leads, and the whole string acts like a single charge, triggered by the first unit. They're very, very cool."

"Can we use them?"

"Oh yeah. I'll take a few with me when I go back."

Echo breathed a long sigh. For so long, she had hoped he would change his mind, but now she accepted it was never going to happen. Military to the core, he always placed duty above self.

From the commissary ruins, he had retrieved several black maintenance coveralls. "Perfect," he said."These will help when I go back to the mine. The dark color will hide me better at night."

Only now was she starting to appreciate how driven this man was. With hope for his crewmates all but gone, his attention was now totally focused on the activities of the aliens back at the mine.

She understood him better now; the more she learned about him, the closer she felt. The thought that he intended to return to the alien compound sent her into a gray 'fug' that clouded her mind and refused to disperse.

Her companion was gentle and attentive, and she enjoyed being with him, but the magic of that first night never resurfaced. Lately, it lacked the urgency, the adrenaline. Always worn-out after working alone all day on the courier ship, his mind was often elsewhere unless she drew him back to the 'here and now'. Aware of his exhaustion, she accepted the situation and pressed on.

***

Barbus Koll grumbled as he peered at the computer screen, examining video from his tame scientists' latest little toy, a drone able to overfly an area without detection.

They had many of these inventions, most of which they came up with in their off-hours. Koll knew he should have reported some of them to Command, especially the gadget that brought down the Terran ship, but there was always time for that in the future. For now, he had more important things to concern him. Specifically, his biggest concern was how to overcome the damage this posting was doing to his career.

For the last year, he had maintained surveillance of the other empty mine-sites along the coast, sending a scout ship once a week for a flyover. He hated such a colossal waste of resources, and so months ago ordered his researchers to find a better way. Their response was the small, virtually silent drone.

Now the result appeared on the screen before him, a drone's-eye image of the main tarmac of the military base. Koll's problem was, the airfield did not appear as deserted as it should. To one side of the apron, beside the disabled Terran ships, stood a shadow outline that could only be human. Reaching for the intercom, he called the barracks. "Brask, get in here now."

Less than a minute later, the frantic officer knocked and entered the room, straightening his uniform as he came in.

"Did you not report," Koll asked, his voice calm and his eyes never leaving the computer screen, "that the two humans were destroyed when you blew up the cabin in the mountains?"

The captain snapped to attention. "Correct, Coordinator,"

"How do you explain this?"

The officer moved to Koll's side and looked over his shoulder. "Ah. Another one. How can that be?"

"How, indeed. Are you sure you killed the others?"

"Positive, Sir. The building contained two clear heat signatures when we fired. There was no possibility of their escape. This must be another, a second refugee from the initial invasion, I expect."

"Why did we not discover it before now?"

"The scout cars are extremely noisy. It would not be difficult for any survivors in the other settlements to hear us coming and hide somewhere our detectors cannot reach."

The coordinator eased back into his chair, for a moment debating how best to deal with the situation. Most of the time, Brask was a good officer, and blaming him for this would achieve nothing. The scientists complained every day about the loss of their specimens to the envoy from High Command, so perhaps a new one for them to play with might be in order.

"Get your team together. Go to the airbase and catch that animal—now."

"Yes, Sir." Brask paused by the door on his way out. "Would it not be more efficient to destroy the place? The two scouts can level it in minutes."

"No, I want this human alive. Besides, I am on strict orders from Central Command to keep the air base intact until they can dispatch a transport carrier to retrieve one of those Terran ships. It is repairable, and they intend to use it for some kind of infiltration project."

With a quick nod, the Captain left, pulling the door closed behind him. Koll turned to gaze out of his window. Another one, he thought. How many of those damnable animals are out there?

Chapter Fourteen

LATE IN THE EVENING Ben ambled into the residence and sat opposite Echo. "It's done," he said with a broad grin. "Maybe not the slickest boat in Fleet, but she's space-worthy, and everything essential works. One of the ground tanks still has enough to see us to a safe system so in the morning I'll re-fuel her. It would be easier to move the ship out on the tarmac, but I'm going to leave her in the workshop. There are some fuel line extensions I can use."

"Why do it inside?"

"Outside she'll be visible to the weekly flyover. The bastards might choose to ignore something they don't consider a threat, but they won't overlook a new vessel sitting here, especially a military one. Besides, if the pump blows I don't want the ship anywhere near it."

"The flyover didn't come this week. How about we roll the ship out, fuel up, and leave?" she asked with one last hope.

Ben reached across to take her hand. "You know I can't do that. I at least have to make an effort to retrieve that research data. Whatever they are working on is, I think, so dangerous it may have serious implications for humanity. Then there's the device they used to knock out my ship. Imagine what would happen to our fleets if those bastards installed one of those on each of their warships."

"Yes, I understand that now. I'm just afraid you'll be caught again. So, what are we going to do?"

"I'll fuel the dispatcher and park her inside the hangar door. When the time comes, we can fire up and roll out under power at a second's notice. Once we are ready I can go back to the Tollean camp, sneak in,—with more care this time—break into the lab, get my crew out if they are still there, and steal the data block if I can. You better stay and guard the plane, in case."

"Not a chance. I'm coming with you."

Ben did not reply. He had expected that response. Anything else would have disappointed him.

"I don't think your crew is still there," Echo said.

For a moment he sat in deep contemplation. "No, most likely not."

After dark Ben dragged a kitchen chair into the room they used for sleeping, and by the light of an oil lantern began pouring through a manual from the maintenance hangar.

"What's the book?"

"Refueling manual. Those pumps haven't run in years, so I'll have to do it manually. That stuff is tricky, so I thought I'd brush up before I try anything."

Echo lay staring up at the mold on the ceiling, giving a loud sigh. Ben put the booklet aside. "Are you alright?"

"No … yes … sorry."

"I know you want to leave this place but everything will be fine, believe me."

"That's not it. I can't do this anymore. If you're killed, I'll be alone again. I'm not sure I can handle that. Not again."

Ben moved across to the bed and pulled her up until they sat facing each other. "Listen, we need to clear something up."

"What?"

"You! You have this stupid notion burned into your brain that you can't cope or survive on your own anymore and that if anything happens to me you'll be helpless. I feel flattered, but that could not be further from the truth."

Echo did not respond, staring at him through blurry eyes.

"Look at the reality," Ben continued. "Before the attack, the human population on this planet numbered about two thousand. Only one survived—you, and you kept yourself alive for years. When those bastards came back you lived off the land, hiding alone in the forest. You had the foresight to set up an emergency hideaway in the caves, and when I got myself shot you killed my attacker and rescued me. When they destroyed the cabin you saved us and then got us to this base. And you've kept us alive and safe while I worked on the ship. I don't possess your hunting and survival skills, and I am way out of my environment here. Without you, I would be dead from starvation by now."

"So…?"

"So you're not helpless at all. Far from it. You are the most persistent and capable woman I've ever met, and that's why I love you. You don't need me—it's the other way around." Ben sat back on his heels and smiled. "You can come with me to the Tollean base, but I want you to stay outside as a backup. If anything happens I might need rescuing again. If I get myself killed you'll survive fine until another ship comes. Take my word for it."

Echo's eyes locked on his in the dim light. "You said you loved me."

"Yes," he said quietly. "I guess I did." He kissed her gently, went back to his chair, and picked up the manual again. "I better finish this."

I don't think so. Echo jumped to her feet. As slow and seductive as possible, she glided over to Ben's chair, took the booklet from his hand and straddled his knees, wrapped her arms around his neck, and peered into his deep, blue eyes.

***

When the dawn light began to appear Echo lay crumpled against Ben, her mind adrift on balmy, nebulous daydreams. She felt safe, more so than at any other time in the last four years.

Before the Tollean attack, no man dared approach even with her permission, not only because of the law—she was a child then and the colony regulations were harsh regarding relationships with minors—but also because she was the daughter of the boss. She believed in all honesty that if any man had touched her, her father would have castrated him.

She found consolation with the boys of her own age who, like her, took little stock in the adults' rules. Popular with them all she let herself become close only to one, but he was no more experienced than she was. Their encounters were fun, but they were only games.

With Ben it was different; it meant something.

As the sun appeared, Echo rose to begin the new day. After breakfast, Ben announced he was going to refuel the ship, and disappeared in the direction of the maintenance hangar. He refused her help with this final chore, explaining the fuel transfer posed considerable dangers after four years of zero maintenance on the facility. With nothing else to do, Echo decided to go for a morning swim, something she had done frequently in the last few weeks.

On the hillside behind the airfield, the pipeline from the dam constantly fed the massive water tank providing water to the base. An overflow drained excess runoff, first into a broad, shallow, concrete bowl forming a meter-deep pond, and then by a channel to a nearby gully.

With no maintenance for years, the surrounding vegetation covered much of the perimeter of the basin giving the appearance of a small forest pool, and what local wildlife there was came there frequently to drink. Periodic overflow kept the water clean, and Echo found it a perfect spot to swim. She loved relaxing in the chill water, looking down through the trees to the airbase. It reminded her of her forest pool at home, and she did not mind sharing it with the small creatures.

By midday, it was almost time to return to the residence. Far below, Ben walked across to the feed-pipe control valves for the single facility still containing fuel. The hoses were gone so the refueling was complete; he had promised the task would only take a few hours and he was good to his word. The now space-worthy ship was safely hidden inside the hangar, the doors firmly closed again.

Propped on the concrete rim Echo gazed in the direction of the distant mountains. Set back from the coastal ridges, the main range in this region was imposing, the tops of the distant peaks snow-capped year round despite the planet's hot climate.

On the far side of the compound, something moved by the entrance. Beyond the damaged sentry post a vehicle came to a stop, then several bulky figures climbed out and strode purposefully through the gate.

Damn, Echo thought. The monsters! Were they aware of her and Ben's presence? At first, she intended to shout a warning, but before words could leave her mouth she stopped and ducked down again. With no chance of getting to her man in time and nothing but a crossbow for defense, she could do little to help him. Yelling would only alert the aliens to her presence.

Her mind flew back to a similar circumstance where she had watched her father die.

Déjà Vu.

Determined to help Ben, she scrambled from the pond and ran down the track towards the back of the airstrip.

Beneath one of the disabled ships the human squatted by the shattered engine cowling and sheltering from the sun. He was completely unaware of Brask and his men. As he turned, an animal net flew towards him through the air.

Brask's guards ran forward as the human collapsed under the weight of the netting, pinned him to the ground then constrained his wrists with shackles before they removed the mesh and marched him away.

The creature wore the black uniform of the ones who once occupied this outpost and looked to be working on one of the ships on the tarmac when he and his men arrived, perhaps in an attempt to make the thing space-worthy. It had been standing in the same spot where first detected by the flyover. Its face seemed familiar, but all these creatures looked the same. The capture had been all too easy. The prisoner dealt with, Brask stood on the administration-building forecourt and cast his eyes around the compound.

He was satisfied that this, like the one back at the compound, was a survivor from the invasion, undiscovered until caught by the new, silent drone. He ran his eyes over the surrounding structures. An early morning flyover detected only a single heat signature on the base, and he was confident the human was alone. A search of the buildings was pointless, and Brask wanted to escape this hellish sun and return to his cool, cozy barracks as quickly as possible. Still, Koll would ask, so he would make a quick inspection.

He ignored the corner hangar and the ordinance bunker. They were secured months ago on Koll's orders, and from a distance appeared to be undisturbed. Not intending to make anything more than a cursory check Brask began to walk a quick circuit of the compound.

Fifteen minutes later Echo stood at the entrance gate as a cloud of dust disappeared in the direction of the town. With the aliens' attention focused on Ben, she had run down the reservoir track and across to the maintenance hangar to retrieve one of the laser rifles. With her newly acquired skill with the weapon, she had been positive she could deal with the soldiers given the advantage of surprise.

She was too late.

Her man was gone, again. The realization numbed her mind, and she wondered how she could have been so stupid. It was her job to keep guard while he worked. The monsters had waltzed in and captured him far too easily, and she cursed herself for failing to prevent it. Squatting on her haunches in the roadway she stared towards the fading dust cloud, furious at her lack of forethought after having been so hard on Ben for the same weakness.

As the reality of the situation materialized she thought back to what Ben had said the previous night, and a sense of resolve began to grow in her mind. She would go after him. She did need him and was determined to rescue him—or die in the process.

Until now, nothing had seemed worth endangering her life. As a child, she had always been protected by her father and dealt with the initial attack on the colony by going into hiding and concentrating on staying alive. Before Ben's arrival, she had never needed to stand up for what she believed in or wanted.

The idea of fighting for anything or anybody other than herself had never occurred to her before, but now she knew she would do exactly that. As far as she knew he loved her, and she was sure she needed and loved him. Perhaps, after all, the needs of another human being could supersede one's safety; risking everything for Ben no longer seemed ridiculous. For now, at least, he was the most important aspect of her existence, and she did not intend to leave him in harm's way without a fight. Her only doubt was whether he would be dead before she reached him, but that was unlikely; it seemed illogical for the aliens to capture him alive and then take him back to their base and kill him. Then again, they did not always behave logically.

On her feet once more, she ran back to the service buildings where an old, still functional, military vehicle sat in one of the ruined garages. Ben had resurrected it to carry gear around the depot, and it would work well enough for her to return to the mine and rescue him—again.

First, she checked the courier. Ben assured her it was space-worthy, and a quick visual inspection seemed to confirm this. The engine pods were closed and the exterior of the vessel appeared complete and functional. In the cabin the control console was sealed, so Echo assumed the re-wiring was finished. Not that she would know either way, but everything looked good.

She could not operate a spacecraft, but having watched Ben in the past she could mimic his actions to power up the console. A few flicks of the array of switches on the overhead lit up the instrumentation. Fuel readouts showed the fuel tanks full, the reactor functioning, and the ship's battery banks at maximum charge.

After several minutes attempting to decipher the mass of data on the screen she decided the life support and computer systems were functional, then realized she had no idea how they worked anyway. With no sure way of knowing she decided to trust Ben. If he said they worked, they did.

Echo opened the hangar doors. The ship sat inside, ready to roll out under power at a moment's notice. "Now all you have to do is take off," she said. "But not yet."

Over the next few hours, she prepared the old vehicle and loaded the recharged laser weapons and the crate of explosive mines from the ordinance store. When she climbed aboard and turned the ignition key, the sun was already dropping towards the surrounding hills.

That the rusty, old machine could travel the coastal track unscathed was doubtful, but Echo determined to keep going as long as she could before abandoning it. The journey involved driving part of the way without lights, but with both moons up and one of them full, she hoped the natural light would be adequate if she took care.

"Okay, bastards," she cursed under her breath. "Prepare yourselves. Here I come!"

Chapter Fifteen

ECHO SCRAMBLED UP ONTO embankment behind the maintenance hangar at the mine airstrip and peered into the growing gloom.

After a long, petrifying drive the previous night, she had arrived in the early hours of the morning. Familiar with the state of the road and its worst sections from traveling the same route several times in the past, she reached her destination without serious incident and hid the vehicle in the dunes below the settlement.

Through the day, she hid in one of the houses, intending to carry out the rescue under the cover of darkness. As night fell once more, she approached the airfield through the forest.

The plan to save Ben relied heavily on a bag of daisy-chain mines. In the late afternoon, she rigged some of the town buildings with charges to create a simple distraction. The timers would trigger once she was inside the compound, and she prayed the explosions would draw enough of the monsters away to make her task easier.

The Tollean ship and the scoutcraft stood on the tarmac ahead. Echo skirted around the edge until level with the parked machines, keeping to the shadows to avoid detection. The larger spaceship sat apart, with the two smaller scouts closer to the administration office.

Most of the field lay in darkness or shadow, with the same single lamp high on a pole, the sole illumination of the area. Crouching by a nearby drum, Echo raised her crossbow and aimed up at the light. The laser rifle slung on her back and the pistol on her hip were both more accurate, but the flash would raise the attention of the monsters.

The arrow flew true, shattering the lamp. Echo hunched down behind the drum and waited, expecting someone would come to check and, with luck, decide it had blown of its own accord. The fixture could not be repaired without a hydraulic platform, and hopefully, the guards would leave the work until morning.

A solitary alien stepped from the office and strolled up to the lamp pole, flashed a torch at the shattered glass on the ground, and up at the remains of the broken fitting. He turned and shouted unintelligible words towards the open door of the building as he swept his torch in an arc around the immediate vicinity.

Echo held her breath as light washed briefly over the spot where the spent crossbow bolt lay; the beam moved on, the shaft unseen. Satisfied all was in order, the alien returned to his refuge, closing the door behind as he entered.

Score one for me, she thought, creeping through the night towards the spacecraft. According to Ben, this ship carried a crew of seven, who in all likelihood would go straight to their posts in an emergency, ready to lift off if necessary. Human crews did that, so perhaps the aliens operated similarly.

Minutes later, several daisy-chain mines sat on the undercarriage, hidden in the landing gear bays, their radio triggers dialed to the first number on the control unit. Echo slipped the transmitter into a pocket of her shorts and moved on. Not long after, each of the two scout cars contained a charge inside the engine cowling behind the cab, set to the second frequency.

"Okay," she said, stealing across the darkened tarmac. "Your turn, bastards".

Other than the hangars and maintenance sheds, all the structures on the airfield and in the mine yard were 'prefabs', standing above the ground on steel supports. Echo crawled under the office block and secured a trio of mines to the central pillars, setting them to the same frequency as the spaceship.

Beneath the crew barracks, she repeated the process, listening to the sounds of footsteps overhead as she worked. *Enjoy while you can*, she thought, as she scrambled out and vanished into the darkness.

The huge drainage pond, overflowing with years of accumulated rainfall runoff, sat at the back of the strip. A high chain wire fence separated the water from the mine apron, and in one place, two massive pipelines ran through a deep trench beneath the barrier. The gap between the twin pipes was sufficient for a body to squeeze through, providing easy access to the compound. Ben took this route during his initial escape; now Echo used it to enter.

Twenty-three separate buildings filled the administration area, mostly storage sheds, workshops, or garages. Of the remainder, the largest were the old assay laboratory, now converted into a research facility by the Tolleani, and the canteen and utilities blocks, both of which now served as barracks.

Echo estimated the number of remaining guards at sixteen, not including the ones already dead at her and Ben's hands. With seven crew members from the ship, three scientists, and the commandant, she counted twenty-seven aliens in total that might require her attention.

Typical of the Tolleani, few were in sight. A closed sentry box by the exit to the town held one, with a second in a similar post at the gate to the airstrip. A third stood on the veranda of the laboratory, uncomfortable with his forced exposure to an environment he detested.

At the edge of the apron, Echo crouched in shadow, watching and waiting. Twenty-three of the small but powerful mines remained in her knapsack from the original thirty-four, and most of these she intended for the barracks and the lab.

The researchers were still at work, light emanating from the single window of her primary target, the laboratory. The only other buildings of interest to her were the commandant's house, the barracks, the antenna shack, and the ordinance store nearer the mine.

Confident that no more of the enemy were active in the vicinity, she crept over to the store and fixed a single charge to the rear wall, hoping it would suffice to set off anything inside.

Underneath the aerial-festooned building Ben blamed for his capture, she fitted several more.

The compound was better lit than the airfield. A floodlight sat outside each structure, several of them illuminating the central concourse. Echo approached with extra care, crawling safe from detection beneath the prefabricated structures.

Under the barracks, she attached a string of 'daisy chains' to the floor beams before moving across to the canteen to repeat the process, setting all the mines in the compound to the third frequency on the radio trigger. The charges would be set off in a strict order to cover her retreat, and these would be the first. The town exploding in flames should cause at least some of the guards to investigate, but she did not intend to take chances.

The settlement was set to burn in thirty minutes, giving her time to string a few mines beneath the commandant's house. Assuming he would leave the town to his subordinates, she hoped he would meet his end in the same place her father had died.

Using the buildings as cover, she crept up to the airstrip gate. In the security post, the alien guard was half-asleep. From behind a stack of pallets, Echo lobbed gravel at the side of the sentry box to draw him out: she needed this route unguarded for the escape.

Curious to see what was going on outside, the guard opened the door and stepped through, stopping short as a crossbow bolt lodged in his neck. Retrieving the shaft, Echo dragged the body back inside and closed the door to hide it from immediate discovery. One down, she thought, vanishing between the nearby buildings.

Last on Echo's list of targets was the laboratory. After their initial capture, Ben and his crew had been confined in a cage inside, and it was logical that he would be there again, assuming he still lived.

The solitary guard still stood uncomfortably at the front. Echo did not want to eliminate him yet for fear of raising an alarm, so rigging the structure with mines would be more difficult. For now, it would suffice to determine Ben's exact location.

A pile of containers lay at the side of the building. As quietly as possible and mindful of the guard's presence just around the corner on the veranda, Echo positioned a small crate near the only side window and climbed up.

The interior was a large, open space at the center of which sat a massive, cylindrical object she took to be the explosive device mentioned by Ben. Only one alien occupied the room, sitting at a desk with his eyes glued to a computer screen. In the corner behind him, Ben sat in a steel-bar cage, the door of which appeared to be fitted with a solid, built-in lock.

Damn, Echo swore. *Where there's a lock, there must be a key.*

Climbing down from her perch, she retreated to a dark corner with a view of the entrance to the lab. The guard maintained his position, unaware of her presence. Echo settled to wait for the first installment of her impending attack.

It amazed her how little attention the aliens paid to their surroundings. She wondered how these creatures could be winning the war, but then realized the guards in this base might not be the best the Tollean Empire had to offer.

Minutes dragged into an eternity as she hid beside an old mine bucket, eyes on the guard. The veranda was well within bow shot, and from her position, she also had a clear line of sight to the front of the commandant's residence and the guard's quarters.

The nightly rain began, a drizzle turning the ground to mud but shielding her from detection as the drops pounded a steady drum roll on the metal roofs of the buildings.

Only meters away, the Tolleani guard stepped back and leaned against the wall of the building, no doubt adding the rain to his litany of miseries as he waited for his duty shift to end.

Without warning, loud eruptions shattered his contemplation, lighting up the darkness beyond the perimeter fence as flames roared skyward from the center of the old town.

Alerted by the explosions, soldiers flooded onto the concourse. From her vantage point, Echo watched the commandant form ten of his men into a squad, then order one to fetch a vehicle. The old, tinder-dry buildings burned like a beacon in the night as the truck rolled through the gate and along the road to the settlement.

Eleven, she thought. Brilliant. That left only five guards remaining. The response was beyond her best hopes, with only a handful of guards left in the compound. The commandant departed with his men; it was a shame, she thought, as she would have liked a shot at him.

The guard on the laboratory veranda stood motionless, watching his remaining fellows take up positions inside the gate, and cursing at the realization his shift would be much longer than expected.

Echo hesitated to shoot him in the back: that was how she took down the alien at the airstrip weeks ago, but she did not feel sufficiently hard-bitten to repeat the exercise without reservation.

The problem dissolved as the Tollean moved to return to his position against the wall, spotting her in the shadows as he turned. His final impression was of a young human woman standing beside a nearby mine bucket, pointing a strange device the likes of which he had never seen before. He was not aware of the approaching crossbow bolt until it hit him in the center of his forehead.

Echo followed the bolt to the lab entrance, slammed open the door, and rushed in. Adrenaline, not unlike she had experienced during the attack on the cabin, flooded through her body, spurring her on to actions she would never have risked before.

The sole alien occupant of the room reacted instantly, leaping from his seat. Recognizing her as human, he launched himself not at her, nor to cover, but towards a massive, open safe not far across the room. Before he could slam it shut, a blast from Echo's laser pistol dropped him to the floor. Within the cage, Ben jumped to his feet and ran to the bars.

"Over here. Am I glad to see you!"

Echo leaped towards the cage. "Keys? Where are they?"

"In the desk—top drawer, left side,"

Seconds later, she flung the door open and launched herself into Ben's arms.

"You're alive. I thought they might have done something to you. What about your crew?"

"Gone, on the cruiser weeks ago, I guess. What were those explosions?"

"I set fire to the town. Half of the monsters jumped on a truck and went down to check it out. This compound is mined too."

"You did that? Brilliant. They'll be back as soon as they figure out no one is down there. What happened to the one outside?"

"Dead."

"Well done. You'd better drag him inside. If they spot the body, we'll be trapped."

"We have to leave, now."

"No. I have things to do first. Get the guard—please?"

"Damn you, Ben." Echo returned to the veranda and dragged the corpse into the room. At the main gate, the remaining guards still looked towards the town, but from another building, two figures were running to the lab. Echo guessed them to be the other scientists.

Without hesitation, she stepped back inside and away from the door, pistol in hand. As the Tolleani burst through the doorway, she fired, cutting them down before they progressed more than a meter or two into the room. Hauling the corpses clear, she pushed the door shut.

"Pretty handy with that thing, aren't you, beautiful?" Ben turned his attention to the interior of the open safe, retrieving a gray object the size and shape of a book. "Here, this is what we want."

"What is it?"

"The computer memory block. Those guys store it in here every night when they finish their work. I'm guessing it contains their research."

"Okay, so now we go?"

"Not yet," Ben said. "I need to fix something first." He waved a hand towards the bulky object in the center of the lab. "Got any mines left?"

"Yes, eight."

"Give those to me, and the rifle, then nip outside and make sure our way is clear. How did you plan we should leave, gorgeous?"

"I thought we might fly. You did say you could operate those little aircraft?"

"Ha, yeah, I think so. You better check the veranda—and there's a guard by the top gate."

"No, there isn't. Not anymore."

Ben grinned as Echo headed for the door and then began setting explosives around the room. Outside, Echo crouched and searched for the four remaining guards. Three of them stood in the drizzle next to the gate, but of the last, there was no sign.

Several large vehicles restricted her line of sight, so she stepped down to maneuver for a better view. Without warning, something connected hard with the back of her head. Daylight turned to darkness as she collapsed face down on the muddy concourse.

Chapter Sixteen

CAPTAIN BRASK CONGRATULATED HIMSELF It was the little one with the long hair. That might be a problem, he thought. He had reported her dead.

Earlier, he had seen two of the boffins run across to the laboratory. Seconds later, two flashes of light came from inside, and the door closed. Laser fire, he thought, leaving his post.

The door had opened again as he approached the building, so he ducked around a corner, ready to attack whoever came out. Standing over the prostrate form, he applauded himself for making a successful capture while his idiot coordinator wasted time down in the town.

Leaping up to the lab door, he made a quick inspection of the interior. Four corpses lay on the floor inside: three scientists and one of the guards. Presumably, the animal had killed them all. No one else was present, and besides the bodies, nothing looked disturbed. The cage was now empty, but the prisoner was not in the room. Brask assumed he had left by the rear door. He did not stay long enough to detect Ben crouching behind the experimental bomb, having planted the last three mines inside the object's casing.

Kneeling beside Echo's unconscious form, Brask picked up the crossbow and examined it for a moment, turning it in his hands. The device appeared to be some kind of primitive weapon, but nothing with which he was familiar. He cast it aside and returned his attention to the main prize.

The pistol in the creature's hand was something he could recognize. He threw it on the veranda, together with a bag of short wooden shafts, no doubt something to do with the other thing, whatever it was.

Grabbing the animal's feet, he dragged it along the concourse to the coordinator's office. This was worth a promotion, but he supposed Koll would claim the credit, as usual. At the very least, it should appease the coordinator for the failure to kill this human in the canyon.

***

How long she remained unconscious, Echo could not tell. When awareness returned, she found herself on the floor of a small, dim room, hands secured behind her back and feet tied with duct tape. A dull light bulb glowed behind a grill in the ceiling. High on the wall was a single, small window. It was dark outside, so still night.

This room was familiar, Echo thought. She had seen it before. It was the storeroom in her father's old office. Her mind flashed back to the times he brought her here as a treat when she was a child.

On one occasion, he left her to her own devices, ordering her to stay put while he dealt with a minor emergency at the mine entrance. Boredom soon set in, and she had begun to explore, peeking around doors and into unseen places. This was one of those rooms, now her prison.

The alien commandant used this building as a residence. The room was chill, the air dry and foul-smelling, conditioned as a refuge for the Tolleani against the outside environment.

Echo lay motionless and fought to compose herself, wondering what had happened. The missing guard from the gate was most likely responsible, bashing her on the back of the head with something hard. She cursed herself for being so stupid as to not check before stepping out of the laboratory. She wondered about Ben. Did they catch him as well? Was he dead? Perhaps he got away.

Her thoughts in turmoil, she wondered why she had come here at all. This was not exactly staying low until rescue, and now she was a captive. If Ben were dead, no one remained to liberate her. *Why did I have to get involved in this?*

Her obsession with being safe no longer seemed realistic. The first real man in her life besides her father, Ben was also her first real lover. As such, he was a big part of her now, and she would have come to his rescue no matter the consequences. So be it.

Determined not to go quietly, she squirmed her way across the floor and pounded at the door with her bound feet. Like everything else at the mine site, the door was a cheap 'prefab', and she fully intended to break through if necessary.

"Let me out of here, you bastards," she shouted as loud as her lungs would allow. "Let me out now. What did you do with Ben?" Repeatedly, she screamed her challenge, smashing at the door until the thin paneling dented and fractured. Finally exhausted, she slumped back, too winded to continue.

Footsteps sounded from beyond the room. A flash of red light flared through the crack under the door, and a key turned in the lock. The door opened, and Ben stood over her, smiling down with a twinkle in his eyes.

"Ben!"

"You finished loafing around? Or should I close the door again and let you sleep?"

"Damn you." Echo spat. "Cut me loose." Her rescuer vanished into the outer room, returned with a knife, and sliced through the tape around her ankles.

"Okay, let's get out of here." Quickly, he removed the ties from her wrists and helped her to her feet.

"How did you find me?"

"The noise you were making, Santa Claus could have found you."

"Santa Claus?"

"Old legend—never mind. Watch out for the body." In the office, Echo stepped over the inert form of her captor, aware now of the significance of the bright flash under the door.

"How long was I in there?"

"Only about ten minutes. I followed you straight over here, waited until our friend was distracted by your yelling, and took him out." He handed her the crossbow and quiver the alien had discarded outside the laboratory.

"Oh God, thank you." The loss of the bow had not entered her mind, but it felt good to have it in her hands once again. Without hesitation, she fitted a bolt. "I thought you were caught, or killed."

"When this moron stuck his head into the lab I was behind the bomb casing. Didn't spot me, but I saw him." Ben let out a little cackle. "I love these guys. They're so convinced of their superiority over us that they don't take anything near the level of care we would in the same circumstances. Without their superior technology, we would be walking all over them by now."

"Yeah, don't get too comfortable with that thought." Echo glanced at the door. "Can we leave, please? The monsters will be back soon. It won't take long for them to figure out there are no invaders down there."

"I think they're already on their way. Vehicle lights pulled out of the town as I came over here. Five minutes … tops."

From the front of the commandant's residence, the airstrip was visible beyond the gateway. Several dim figures stood in the darkness by the crew barracks with weapons in hand, looking down towards the camp. The spacecraft navigation lights were on.

"Standing orders, I expect," Ben said. "They must be able to see us, but they won't interfere in anything happening down here, and they'll protect their boat at all costs. The ship always comes first. The other crew members will be preparing to lift off if necessary."

"They might be in for a shock," Echo muttered under her breath.

"You mined that as well? Brilliant." Ben's eyes shone with admiration as he kissed her on the lips. "I love you more every minute."

"We can't go that way," she said. "I didn't plan for them to be standing there."

Careful to stay out of sight of the guards at the front gate, they crept across the town to the trench where the pipes led under the fence, and made their way to the top of the earth barrier between the pumping pond and the airstrip. The mound gave a clear view of both the compound and the landing field. Echo removed the trigger device from her pocket.

Ben crawled up beside her. "You set the mines on radio control? The ones in the lab are on timers. I didn't know what you were doing."

"Radio, yes. I want them to go off at the right time. How long before the laboratory goes up?"

"Not until we are well away from here, I hope. I'm not sure what their bomb does, but I don't want to be anywhere close when those charges go up. We need to be well away first."

"Oh, I think we can do that."

Ben rolled over and flashed a grin. "So, we steal a scout ship?"

"Are you positive you can operate them?"

"Yeah, I think so. When the guards captured me, they had one of them waiting beyond the town. They used vehicles to approach the base so we wouldn't hear them coming, but the guard leader used the scout to get me back here quickly. I watched them working the controls on the way back, and I'm pretty sure I can fly it."

"Good, so we go back to our ship. It's ready to take off—I think."

Ben stretched across and kissed her again before turning his attention back to the compound. Inside the main gate, the truck drew to a halt on the concourse. Guards spilled from the rear tailgate as the commandant stalked across to his office.

"The dear boy is going to be pissed when he finds his crony dead on the floor. When are you planning to blow the place?"

"Any minute…" Echo turned the dial on the radio control to frequency three. Seconds later, a roar of anger arose from the camp, and guards started running towards the commandant's residence. A siren began to shriek in the night.

"And … now."

Echo closed the switch, and the night erupted, blooming into the closest thing to hell so fast it was barely possible to comprehend. The barracks disintegrated in a fountain of blue-green flame, sections of the roof flying into the air to come crashing down on the surrounding buildings. On the forward side, the wall blew out, enveloping the truck and several of the alien guards in flames.

"Their armory, I'll bet," Ben said. "You probably put your mines right under it."

Closer to their observation point, the office erupted, its flimsy structure shattered to incandescent matchwood. The canteen and the antennae shed also exploded, sending clouds of flame, smoke, and splinters flying skyward. The ordinance store vanished in a fireball that covered the entire apron area outside the entrance to the mine itself. Of the major structures, only the laboratory remained intact, its roof littered with pieces of burning debris.

"That will go off in about half an hour if the fires don't get it first," Ben explained.

"What if they find the charges?"

"They won't be looking. I put some inside the bomb casing and stowed the rest in dark corners under the benches and in cupboards. Everyone who knew we were inside is dead. Look over there."

He motioned towards the spacecraft not far away on the tarmac. No longer standing near the gate watching, the remaining crew were climbing into the ship as quickly as possible. A solitary figure exited the barracks and dashed to the main building, weapon in hand.

"I think I miscounted," Echo muttered as the alien disappeared. "Doesn't matter." She turned the dial on the radio control to the first frequency and prepared to activate the next set of charges.

"Wait," Ben placed a hand over hers. "Where exactly on that thing did you put the mines?"

"On the landing gear, beneath the wings."

"Shit! Don't hit the trigger yet. Those fins have massive built-in fuel tanks; when they go up, they'll blow everything here to kingdom come, including the scout cars. Escape first, big bang later."

Beyond the earth embankment, the ship's engines started to wind up. Of the figure seen entering the office, there was no sign.

"Let's go." Ben jumped to his feet, grabbed Echo by the hand, and ran down the slope with her close behind. The scout machine resembled a hover car, with a huge bubble dome at the front and four small jet engines set on pivots, two to a side, each one pointed at the ground. Echo climbed into the forward passenger seat as Ben fumbled around beside his seat. Seconds later, he pulled a key from a small pocket and held it up, grinning.

"No different than us. Keep your eyes open until we are away." The small craft roared to life as he pressed the ignition.

Immediately, a figure appeared at the administration-building doorway with his rifle in hand. In the dim light, he seemed unsure of who had started the engines of the scout car, but with no idea what was happening, he withheld fire.

Pulling back on the control stick, Ben launched the car into the air. Echo grasped the seat frame; the sides of the cockpit were open, and she had never been in any kind of aircraft before, much less one where nothing stood between her and a long fall. For a brief moment, she remained frozen until the little craft began to move forward.

"You okay?" Ben asked, guiding the scout out over the stream and the forest beyond.

"Yeah ... Fine."

"Good. You can hit that switch anytime now, but put your seat belt on first."

Seconds later, the airfield erupted as both spacecraft and administration buildings lifted skyward. Propelled by the violent eruption of the fuel tanks, the doomed ship flipped and dropped back to the airstrip in an intense fireball.

Chapter Seventeen

KOLL STARED IN HORROR towards the airstrip, now lit by the flames from the burning ship and buildings. A wave of fury surged through his gut. This should not be happening. His base was under assault from an unseen force, and nobody had any idea who the attackers were.

Except him.

The escape from the office explosion had been the closest of his life. On his return from the town Brask's body confronted him on the floor of the office, and without hesitation he triggered the general alarm and called the guards. A solid hammer blow knocked him to the ground as he stepped back outside, the building behind him exploding along with several others. Stunned but uninjured he had dragged himself to his feet and staggered to the center of the concourse.

Up at the landing field, two small figures had run towards the surveillance scouts. Although they were only just visible from the light of the burning compound and the spacecraft landing lights, Koll did not doubt their identity. One scout craft had lifted off followed seconds later by the disintegration of the airfield buildings and the destroyer rising into the air on a column of red flames and black smoke.

Many of the structures about the compound lay in ruins, and several of the guards still at the truck had been lost. Koll expected the casualties to include the scientists, who spent all their off-work hours lounging around in the conditioned comfort of the now-destroyed barracks.

A soldier ran towards him from the laboratory, the only major building left unscathed. The guard jumped to attention. "Four dead in there, Coordinator, the three boffins, and one rating."

"The prisoner?"

"Gone, Sir."

Koll refrained from tearing strips of the guard, turning his gaze back to the airstrip. The animals could only be going to one place, and they would pay for this atrocity. "Follow me." With a quick check that his pistol was still in its holster, he started at a jog towards the sentry post.

There was little to console him as he ran through the unguarded gateway, finding nothing but devastation. He was sure this meant the end of his career; he would be lucky to avoid the slave markets unless he could find a way to divert the blame elsewhere. How could this happen? You idiot, Brask.

On the field ahead, the remaining scout car lay at an angle, toppled on its starboard engine pods by the force of the exploding spacecraft. Plated with heavy armor to withstand ground attack, the craft had suffered little damage. "Get that thing upright," he ordered as the guards rushed up behind. "I want it flying, now!"

***

Hands firmly grasping the seat, Echo fought to keep calm as the scout flew higher over the mountain ranges. She had never had her feet off the ground before, and now, only inches from a sheer drop of several hundred meters, her stomach churned in threatened rebellion. Eyes closed, she battled to regain control.

With the ordeal almost over and disbelief setting in, she felt sickened by her actions. The creature she had become was loathsome to her. Only a few years ago she had been a child trying to find her way in the only life available to her. Now, after years of surviving alone, she was an adult with a man she loved, but for his sake, she had become a killer responsible for the Gods knew how many deaths. The thought horrified her despite Ben's advice not to think that way.

As he glanced across, Ben knew instinctively what was troubling her. He had felt the same way following his first military engagement. "Remember what I said. Look at them the way you do the animals you killed to survive."

"These are intelligent beings," she shouted over the roar of the engines. "Even if they are our enemies, it's not the same."

"It can be if you choose. This is a war and those bastards are doing their best to destroy us. You did your bit for our side, so now you're a soldier. You saved my life again, and I'm never going to be able to repay you."

"You're safe; that's enough. Get me off this planet."

"My pleasure. The blast should have disabled the other scout, so I doubt if they can follow us. Good job with those mines."

"There are still the ones in the laboratory and two more."

"Two more? Where did you put them?"

"One on each of these scout ships, just in case. I set them to a different channel."

"Shit." Ben grinned nervously, concentrating on his flying. "Clever, but don't trigger them yet."

"How long until we reach the base?"

"A couple more minutes. I don't want to fly this thing too fast; I'm not familiar with it. The courier ship is ready to go so we should be able to take off straight away."

The scout jolted without warning and Echo lurched towards the side opening, prevented from falling out by her safety harness. "What in the Hells was that?"

"Felt like a blast hitting the undercarriage," Ben gasped, focused on his piloting. "I guess the other scout wasn't damaged as much as I hoped."

"We're being chased?"

"Looks like it. They must have flown like maniacs to catch up, but they're right behind us." With the second vessel closing the gap Ben jerked the control stick and jogged to one side then back again, doing his best to dodge their pursuer's fire. He flew lower as he lined up with the air base ahead.

Echo hung on as Ben swerved the scout once again. "Do you think we can make it?"

"You bet we can…"

In a blaze of intensity, the sky dissolved in overpoweringly brilliant light. Far behind, the experimental device had exploded, triggered by the mines inside its cowling. Incomplete, untested, and detonated in the wrong way, it reacted not as intended but like a normal bomb with nuclear force.

The blast flowered in a blinding ball of radiance expanding in all directions, followed by a wave of heat that washed over the forest-clad mountainsides, reducing the trees to ash. From the center of the conflagration, a hemispherical bubble of pure force ballooned outwards, destroying everything in its path.

Almost exhausted by distance, the remnant wall of energy reached the pursuit scout first, slamming into the tiny aircraft like a solid wall. An expert flyer, Koll battled to compensate for the blow, heading off at a tangent as he wrestled his craft back to equilibrium.

By the time the shock wave hit the lead scout, it was lined up for a landing on the airstrip, now only a kilometer ahead. With less experience than his pursuer, Ben fought to keep the alien ship level as they barreled towards the tarmac. Weaker now, the wall of destruction rolled past, sweeping over the air base with little remaining strength.

"Hang on," Ben said. "This is going to be rough." Seconds later the scout thudded to the ground and skidded out of control over the hard surface, streams of sparks flying from the landing gear as it slid and spun sideways into the buildings. Echo closed her eyes again and hung on, convinced she would die but powerless to do anything to prevent it. Focused on the scream of the skids she waited for the final, inevitable crash.

The car stopped hard up against the side of the same building—now leaning at an angle from the force of the blast—that they had lived in for weeks while they repaired the dispatcher. Echo opened her eyes again as Ben climbed from the battered cockpit.

"Out, now." he cried. "This thing could burn at any minute."

Echo unclipped the safety harness, tumbled out of the ship, and scrambled to her feet. Ben was at her side in seconds, taking her by the arm and turning in the direction of the maintenance hangar.

"Not as good as my last landing. We need to go before they come back." Grasping her hand, he urged her on as they ran past the disabled Federation ships. The roar of the pursuing craft assailed their ears as it glided in a broad arc around the field, positioning for an attack.

Enough of this, Echo thought as she stopped, took a deep breath, and turned to face their attacker.

"What in the Hells are you doing?" Ben yelled, turning back.

"I'm ending this."

Sliding a hand into her pocket, she grasped the radio control unit, turned the dial, and pressed the switch one more time.

Across the tarmac, the wrecked scout shattered with a resounding clang as the single mine within detonated. The cab flew high into the air above the roof of the building, ejecting a sheet of flame as the fuel tanks ruptured.

High above, the pursuing craft jerked as the tail section blew away, then flipped and dropped to the surface with a loud crash. Seconds later, it too exploded.

Ben grabbed Echo by the arm again and pulled her towards the hangar. "Tough little buggers to kill aren't they!"

The failing force of the first blast was sufficient to knock Koll's ship into a spin, but using all his skills—as a flyer, he was without peer—he struggled to jockey the little craft back on an even keel. No sooner had he done so than something else slammed into him. The second shock tore the scout apart and sent the wreckage tumbling. Instinct kicked in as he flicked the release on his safety harness and launched himself out of the cab seconds before it crashed.

Prone on the ground, Koll struggled to recover. Shooting pains shot up his legs and through a shoulder; he could neither stand, nor move without pain, but at least he was alive. Motionless, he peered with blurred vision through blood-smeared eyes at the departing humans and realized he had failed.

For a split-second he wondered about his gunner, and then dismissed the thought; the fool was not important. Braced against the pain Koll slid his hand down to his hip and withdrew his pistol from its holster. Those animals would come for him, and he would be ready for them.

Always, he had considered these creatures a worthless annoyance, but now he understood that was not the case.

The two humans inside the hangar were without doubt the spacer who had escaped weeks earlier and the damned animal from the mountains behind the base. His subordinate had assured him they were dead, but not so.

A horrifying truth flooded into his mind.

Brask's fault. All Brask's fault.

Now free, the humans would soon come to kill him, but it no longer mattered. Instinctively aware of what had hit his scout the first time, he knew his men and ships were gone and he was alone, stranded, and seriously injured. The blast had destroyed all evidence of the events of the past few months and unless a rescue arrived in the next few hours, he would die on this airfield.

A sudden sound at the hangar drew his attention. The main door stood wide open and the roar of engines reverberated from inside. Koll's heart sank as a sleek, dark shape emerged from the shadows of the interior. The Terran ship, looking every bit space-worthy, rolled out on the tarmac, its engines whining as power mounted.

"No," Koll gasped. He had seen that ship in pieces. How could those animals have put it back together?

The spacecraft rose in a cloud of dust, hot exhaust washing across the field as it slid up and away toward the clouds. As the blast eased, Koll lifted his head and looked up at the speck receding in the distance.

This was not over yet, he thought.

Chapter Eighteen

ECHO FLOATED TOWARD colossal, blue and white marble on the main screen. She had never seen her world, or any other for that matter, from space. Once again, she found herself unprepared; the sight was overwhelming.

At first, the take-off acceleration forced her back into her seat and terrified her, but with the ship now in zero-gravity, it was over. The nausea had hit the minute they reached space, her stomach threatening retaliation for the third time since takeoff.

"You'll be fine," Ben said, in his element now. His strength and calmness reassured Echo enough for her to be able to view the situation with a clearer mind.

Still fighting to keep her stomach in check, she examined her surroundings. Built for utility and not comfort, the ship's interior was sparse and less than inviting.

Doesn't matter … I'm free, finally, she thought.

Settling into one of the seats in the cockpit, she contemplated the tiny living space, little more than a dinette and a small galley. Further aft, Ben hovered over four coffin-like sleeping and hibernation compartments, two on each side of the cabin. A door at the back led to a bathroom and then to a storage bay, both of which Echo had already checked out.

The bay was empty except for what supplies she had been able to prepare while Ben had been repairing the ship, and had loaded before setting off on his rescue. This was going to be a long ride, Echo thought.

"We're safe now?"

"Yes. At least, no one is left to chase us. That device went off like an old-style nuclear weapon; there can't be any survivors."

Echo turned her attention back to the screen. The ship was approaching the end of its first orbit of the planet, and the site of the recent cataclysm stretched out below. An irregular, pale-gray patch centered on her old home extended across the ridges almost to the next town, marking the extent of the blast. The forests, her beloved trees, no longer existed, a long smudge of dark smoke extending across the face of the world almost to the snow-capped peaks of the main range.

"Where do we go now?"

"We return to my base. This boat should be able to take us home without incident."

"Will we be there soon?"

"It takes time, even with the wormholes. About four weeks." Ben saw Echo's alarm. "Don't worry. We have hardly any supplies, so we'll sleep most of the way. Those sleeping bays,"—he nodded his head towards the rear of the cabin —"are stasis chambers. We climb in and wake up when we arrive home. The computers will keep us safe, and the time will fly by."

"What if we're attacked on the way?"

"Unlikely. You would be surprised how hard ships are to find in open space. The only time we can be detected is while entering or leaving a wormhole. On the off-chance the Tolleani do spot us, the ship will wake us in time to evade them. Nothing to worry about."

Nothing to worry about, Echo repeated in her mind. Now that she was safe, her mind was working overtime. All she ever knew—her family, her friends, her town, her entire existence—was gone. No home, no life, no purpose, nothing but the clothes she wore, her crossbow, and Ben.

"What about us?"

"Us?" Reaching across, he grasped her hand in his own.

"I … I don't … I want us to stay together. You said you loved me."

"I do. No way am I letting you get away. I'm never going to find another like you. What man wouldn't want a gorgeous, kick-ass partner?" For a moment, they sat in silence.

"What are we going to do when we reach your base?"

Ben reached down beside his seat and lifted the small data block taken from the Tollean laboratory. "First up, we give this to the authorities. With any luck, details of both the bomb and whatever downed my ship are on here. You're going to be famous, you know."

"Famous?"

"Yeah. If I am right about this disk, it may be a turning point for the war."

"And us?"

"There could be a promotion in this for me, and if so, it will include certain privileges. Somewhere to live outside the base might be nice—a place of our own."

"What if they send you away again?"

Ben squeezed her hand. "Well, as long as the war continues, I am still an officer, and I will be for some time. I go where I'm sent. If they transfer me to another base, you come with me, assuming you want to."

"Yes, unless you find another gorgeous, kick ass partner."

"How likely is that?" he asked with a grin.

Echo settled back in her seat. The future looked brighter, her mind finally at ease. She was sure she loved Ben, but wondered how she would feel about him if not for all they had been through together.

Her father once told her danger made strange bedfellows; now she understood his meaning. Life would be different. She was not sure how, but better. She was uncertain how she would cope with normality after the last four years.

The old life she had anticipated was nothing but a distant memory, but a new path was opening. Where it would lead, she had no idea, but Ben was a beginning. Echo knew that deep down, and despite Ben's opinion of her survival abilities, she was still the seventeen-year-old child who watched the initial attack on Corros. In many respects, she had a great deal to learn and a lot of growing up to do, but now, at least, she had the time. Maybe, with Ben's help…

The remnants of her childhood slipped out of sight on the video screen. Echo let out a loud sigh.

"If they keep sending you out on missions, what am I going to do?"

For a moment, Ben studied her. "I imagine you could do anything," he replied, a broad smile on his face. "I can only imagine."

End

Author's Note

DID YOU ENJOY 'SOLITUDE'S END?
IF SO, YOU CAN MAKE A BIG DIFFERENCE.

Dear Reader:

Reviews are the most powerful tool I have when it comes to getting attention for my books, and help bring them to the attention of other readers. They also increase the chances of the better review and promotion sights picking the book up, and increase a book's visibility on major book sales sights.

If you've enjoyed Solitude's End and have five minutes to spare, I would be eternally grateful if you could spend a minute or two leaving a review (an honest one, and as short as you like) on the book's review page at your favorite bookstore or on GoodReads.

Thank you.

Mike Waller

EXCERPT - DARK WORLD

BEN LET HIS MIND wander as memories of Echo drifted through his consciousness. A vague smile flickered across his lips as he pictured her angelic smile. Why she stayed with him was beyond comprehension, but she did, and Ben counted his blessings.

He remembered how she ran her fingers across the ever-present stubble on his chin and along the line of strange characters tattooed down his right flank. He knew those characters fascinated her, but in all the time he had know her their meaning had remained a mystery. She believed they held a great secret, perhaps a love or tragedy from a past time, and he did not want to disillusion her with the knowledge they were meaningless.

He remembered also the place where they first laid eyes on each other. *Corros! The prospector's cabin, that's where.* High in the forested mountains of Echo's home world, the old cabin was warm and welcoming. *We destroyed that place. The forest, the mine, the town … gone … forever!*

An urgent buzzing sounded at the edge of his awareness. The alarm wormed its way into his brain, the irritation growing louder and more persistent with each passing second. He continued to stare up at the dull, grey ceiling in the master's cabin of his new ship as the noise drove him from his contemplation.

After escaping from the now Tolleani controlled planet, he and Echo were at first never apart, but with his resumption of duty and reassignment it was over a month since they had last been together.

Their escape had been a year ago, and prior to that Echo spent four years alone, the sole survivor of an invasion that killed every other colonist in the planet's three mining settlements. Sent to investigate the chance of re-taking the colony, Ben's spacecraft crash-landed when attacked by an unknown prototype weapon, at an alien research base occupying one of the mine sites. Not long after capture, he escaped from the Tolleani and stumbled upon Echo's refuge in the forested canyons of the surrounding mountains. Only with her help did he survive. Twice, she saved his life.

Now they were together. The knowledge that she would wait for him until this mission ended did little to ease the pain of separation by light years of space.

Irritated by the rude interruption, he yawned and scratched at the stubble on his chin. A slap on the intercom screen stopped the annoying buzz.

"Yes, Jerry?"

"Sorry to disturb you, Cap," a voice replied. "A distress call just came in on the common band. Thought you ought to know."

Ben stood, lurched and tumbled into the opposite bulkhead. The mission was several weeks old now, but after months either in hibernation or planet bound, returning to the routine of life in a zero gravity tin can required a long readjustment. Every lapse of attention resulted in a new mystery bruise.

*　*　*

The first officer Jerry Bayer was the only other person on the control deck. With a quick nod of acknowledgement, Ben turned to the command console.

"Status?"

"The gateway to the *Arpeche* System is ahead, Captain. We're twenty hours from the jump point, and the ship sending the signal is sitting in front of the gate."

Ben floated into the captain's chair and studied the screens. "Hmm … fine. Keep monitoring it, and keep your wits about you. We've had a few unexplained disappearances in this sector recently, so keep your eyes open."

This ship was his first command, granted soon after promotion to captain. Less than six months passed after their return to *Cymbel 3* before he received his bars and orders. With the war in full swing and humanity losing, the commission was inevitable, and with it came command of a brand new destroyer. Ben gave most of the credit to Echo; without her, he would have died long ago, somewhere in the wasteland now covering the site of her childhood home.

Even now, a modified version of the Tollean device used to bring his last vessel down was being installed on Fleet's front-line ships. No reports were in yet on the weapon's effectiveness, but with the first fitted little more than a month ago, that did not surprise Ben. Word was slow to travel in space. This destroyer carried one of the units, still untested in action.

Give it time, he thought. The research Echo and I stole will bring an end to this war, or at least a compromise.

Jerry interrupted his thoughts. "Captain, the signal isn't from a Fleet vessel, but it's certainly a distress call. Someone's in trouble."

"What do we know?"

"There's a Terran vessel, a "CS34" class, sitting in front of the gateway. Human, not Tollean. The request is on the general band, but no security codes."

"Civilian? Okay, send an acknowledgement. Get me a visual as soon as you can."

The image on the monitor was a short-haul freighter, old and worn but with no visible damage. It drifted at the middle of a region of empty space otherwise referred to as a gateway, containing the entrance to the Arpeche 497 wormhole. On the side of the hull, faded and flaked paint spelled out the number AF10739.

"The computers have no record of that registration, Captain," Jerry said. "Must be from an unaligned planet." Dozens of worlds throughout the occupied galaxy had either left the federation of humanity or never joined. Many of them had fallen to the Tolleani, unnoticed beneath the radar.

"Freighter AF10739, this is Fleet destroyer G4973, Ben Teague commanding. Please advise your situation."

Several minutes later, a soft, feminine voice responded. "Captain Teague, Julia Ellis here. You cannot imagine how happy I am you're here. Thank you for responding."

"My pleasure, Captain Ellis. What is your status?"

"My engines are down. An explosion in the engineering module occurred as we exited the gate from *Arpeche*. The damage is repairable but my engineer is injured. I would appreciate the help of yours, and medical attention for mine."

Ben acknowledged without a moment's hesitation. Not responding to a distress call in space was contrary to regulation, and had severe consequences. "My engineering officer will cross with our paramedic as soon as we rendezvous."

"Would linking our ships be possible?" Ellis asked. "My casualty is in a critical condition and we have no facilities. His leg is broken, so we can't get him into a suit. I have a transfer pod, but I need your inter-lock tube to bring him across to you."

"Sorry, no. You're not broadcasting an approved security code. Fleet regulations do not permit a link with any vessel unless it identifies itself in the correct manner."

"My apologies, Captain. This ship is an unaligned freelance freighter and not part of the Federation. We've not been home for three months and don't have your codes, so we can't verify ourselves. Perhaps your people can check us over and then you might agree to a connection?"

For a moment, Ben pondered the situation. To give help in a medical emergency was obligatory under Fleet regulations, but he would not put his command at risk. "I'll let you know when we come alongside. Stand by."

Hours later, the old freighter drifted beside them in space, less than a hull's length separating the two ships.

"Looks harmless enough," Jerry said. "Doesn't appear to be any visible damage, and no weapons. I have six heat signatures inside, one prone."

"Send Raj and Miko across and we'll wait for their report."

Thirty minutes later the voice of Ben's medical officer Miko came over the speaker. "Captain, everything appears in order here. The patient's femur is broken; he has serious blood loss and is unconscious. We need to set up the tunnel to bring him over so I can stabilise him and repair the leg. This ship has no facilities."

Ben noticed more than usual stress in Miko's voice. "You are aware Fleet regulations do not allow me to approve a direct connection until I am satisfied there is no threat?" he said.

"Yes sir. The regulations also require we help wherever possible when lives are at risk. This man will die unless he gets attention." Miko's voice was forced, and showed obvious concern.

"Can you do it there?"

"No. The fracture I can fix, but he needs transfusions. I need my medical bay, Benjamin, please. Regulation 973 requires I help this man." Once again Ben could hear the tension in her voice.

"Have you checked the ship?"

"Yes, everything is ten-ten. Raj is heading back to the engine module now. Benjamin, it's just what you would expect of a surveyor."

Ben looked across to his second in command. "Miko is upset about something, wouldn't you say?"

"Distraught, I guess. Doesn't surprise me. The worst she gets on this boat is vitamin deficiency and headaches; now she has a potential critical. She called you Benjamin."

"She's never addressed me by my name before, much less Benjamin. Always *Captain*. And ten-ten? Have you ever heard of regulation 973?"

Jerry shook his head. "Can't find it on the computers. She's definitely trying to tell us something."

A direct connection with an unknown ship was contrary to orders and an enormous risk, and Miko's words indicated there was a problem she could not talk about. If anything happened, the result would be loss of command for Ben. According to his medical officer there was a life in danger, and other regulations dictated that help must be provided. The vessel was of human origin—that at least, was clear. Ben considered the options. Dammed if I do…

"Alright," he said, "we'll set up now, Miko." The risk, he decided, was unavoidable. "Captain Ellis will cross with you, plus the patient and Raj. Nobody else. As soon as you are aboard, I'll meet with her. You will all remain in the bay and I'll come to you."

"Yes, Sir."

Ben switched to the internal intercom. "Bayliss and Mahib, get down to the airlock. Set up the link tunnel as quickly as possible, carry your side arms and be wary. The visitors may not leave the bay under any circumstances. You will keep them under guard until I get there." Flicking the intercom off, he turned to Jerry. "We need to get our people out of there. I have serious concerns about this."

Something troubled him about the whole situation. The prospector showed no obvious sign of external damage, but Ellis had explained there was an isolated explosion inside the engine room. The scanners confirmed the engines were cold.

Uncomfortable with the docking tube, he was even more so with leaving a civilian spacecraft helpless and an unconscious, injured man without hope. Miko's speech also concerned him; clearly, she had been attempting to tell him something under duress.

She has never addressed me by my name before.

"On their way now," Jerry said. "Four persons crossing: Miko with the patient in a capsule, Raj assisting and Captain Ellis."

Ben watched on the intercom as the arrivals approached the airlock and moved into the bay. He rose and glided back towards his cabin, thinking it a coincidence the disabled ship should malfunction right on the entrance to the wormhole, the one place in the vastness of space with a guarantee of early rescue. Again, Ellis had an explanation, that they had just exited the gateway.

He retrieved his side arm. With that, and with armed crew in the docking bay, he was at least prepared if anything went wrong. Returning to the bridge, he was about to head back to the bay when the hatch to the control deck burst open.

A middle-aged male wearing Raj's pressure suit floated through, a laser pistol in his hand. Behind him a woman, also armed and threatening, and wearing Miko's pressure suit, pulled herself through the opening.

The man holding the gun was tall and rangy, with blonde, thinning hair and a stubbled chin. Green eyes glittered in the cockpit lights as he glanced around, an almost euphoric look on his face. Focusing his attention on Ben, he licked his lips as if savouring a tasty dish or a fine wine. "Please stay in your seat, Captain," he said, "and keep your hands away from the console."

"Who in the Hells are you? Where is my crew?"

"Your engineer and paramedic are safe on board my ship. My worthy associates are attending to your men in the bay. Oh, and your vessel is now my property."

The woman, most likely the same who identified herself as Captain Ellis, smiled as her companion spoke. The man peered around the cabin again, a broad Cheshire-cat grin spread across his face.

"A Fleet destroyer." he crowed. "I am going to find this so useful."

To continue reading 'Dark World', check out the book at your favourite online bookstore.

OR

https://www.mikewallerauthor.com/dark-world-book-2-of-echos-way

ABOUT THE AUTHOR

Mike Waller is a writer of Science Fiction and Space Opera adventures, including the 'Echo's Way' stories and other stand-alone works. He currently lives in Queensland, Australia.

Mike's online home is at:

www.mikewallerauthor.com

Join Mike Waller's Readers' Group for a free book.

You can connect with him on Facebook at:

www.facebook.com/AuthorMikeWaller/

You should email him at

mike.waller@mikewallerauthor.com.

Mike answers every email received.

ALSO BY MIKE WALLER

ECHO'S WAY Books

SOLITUDE's END - Book 1 of "Echo's Way"

DARK WORLD - Book 2 of "Echo's Way"

ENEMY ALLY – Book 3 of "Echo's Way"

The FALCON Trilogy

FALCON's CALL

FALCON's GHOST

FALSON'S BANE

OTHER

HAWK: HELLFIRE